Table of Contents

Introduction

Birthday Wishes

The Purple Eyed Opossum of Preston Memorial

#NoBadVibes

Name Day

The Merry Dancers

Transformations

Voice of Reason

From the Other Side

Stitches

The Lizard and the Dove

Magical Man-eater Makeover

The Two Brothers

Recollection

When a Scoundrel Calls

Rosemary Rosemary

They are of the Stars – An Introduction by the Author

Fresh Beginnings

The Promises of Ghosts

Introduction

Firstly, thanks for purchasing this. We're raising money for a Neonatal bereavement team who do a lot of work very quietly to support bereaved families. And as I've learned, they don't stop caring once you leave the hospital, so this is my thank you to Catriona and the team at Forth Valley Royal Hospital and the NICU team at the Victoria Hospital.

You don't have to be Sherlock to have figured out there's more to the story here. I won't bore you with the details. When I started this journey, it was a means of processing what I needed, a way to make it through the day and then another, then another. I had to try to make things better, manufacture a silver lining. My vision for this anthology came from the months we spent in a NICU, panicked and exhausted, it's a world you never want to know and when you do you're just not prepared for it. There's no way to prepare for it. But within days, you know the difference between a SATS alarm and a BRADY alarm. You lose your fear of handling tiny bodies and instead marvel at watching the neonatal development that should have been happening quietly in the dark, happen in the light. It's strange and amazing and completely disorientating and one of the hardest things is figuring out when/how/if it's going to end.

Because there will be days when it feels like it just won't. But it does, and suddenly this place you've been desperate to leave becomes the only place you think your kid will be safe but you're on your way home and it looks like EVERYONE has a cold and you've heard this flu season is going to be rough and RSV is filling the children's' ward and...a new set of stresses begin.

What I needed at the time was something to hold on to. A way of knowing what the path ahead of me looked like and a guide to safely walking it. Because something Earth shattering happened and what I lost was the sense of safety. That belief that no matter what, everything would be ok. Apologies, Reader, this isn't such a guide. If I'd found one, I promise I'd share it, but every journey is so different. And this isn't just for the NICU but for everyone going through things that shake you to your core. I wanted to help, but sometimes there's nothing to do but be there, and stand beside someone. So, with the help of my dear friends, we decided to send through time and space, from our hearts to yours, a hand.

Take it, and for a moment, let your mind go somewhere else. Rest within our kooky pages. The stories within aren't meant to 'teach' you anything. But our fervent hope is that while you're reading, for just those few moments everything really is ok. Rest and gather your strength because whatever you're going through is probably harder when you're tired. Recharge and start again. Because you'll cope, you'll keep moving and, in a year, things will look different. 5 years, they'll be even more different. At some point, you might find you're excited to find out how different they are. I'm not there yet but I've heard it's coming and to quote my favourite wizard, 'that's an encouraging thought'.

It took me 16 months to start proper counselling and at the time of writing I'm only three months in. I've been told that we as a society are horrible at handling grief, that we all put some kind of time limit on it. After about 6 months, if people see you smiling and laughing and joking, they assume you're ok now. It's all better. For me, that's just not the case. I'm never ok, but I'm not *not* ok. I don't have the words (believe it or not!) to really answer the question 'how are you?' anymore. I'm actually, incredibly lucky and blessed. I'm unfathomably broken. I can't watch the Property Brothers anymore and I'm surrounded by friends and family who show up at a moment's notice and just stand beside me. Or draw for me or write for me. They show up. And now we're showing up for you.

Whoever has this book right now, whatever your pain, we're standing beside you. We're your shadows on a road that feels empty and alone. Within this book you might giggle, you might cry, you might think we've all lost the plot. But we hope you enjoy it, because you're allowed to (and you're allowed to feel guilty for not feeling horrible. But a decent cuppa should temper that).

Anyway, forgive my rambling. Everything else in here has far more direction I assure you. I suppose all that's left to say is, whoever you are and for whatever reason you're here, thank you for reading.

   Love, Sam

   ✦

Birthday wish

Samara Wright

You've got all the words there. I can get what you're trying to say, but it's not that simple. It won't translate one for one. I never said learning Japanese was going to be easy. It's not related to English at all. You shouldn't try to think in translation, taking every English word and replacing it before tackling the grammar. Languages live; they breath meaning and nuance instead of air, but they grow and change right along with us. Take *natsukashii,* another word that doesn't translate directly. I know, I know. Another one. But this one is used often enough it's worth studying.

If you're thinking it means nostalgic, you're close. That's definitely one facet of it. But think of what nostalgic means. A sentimental feeling, a longing for the past. Something desired, something dear. And something missed. That's a better definition for *natsukashii*.

Think of the fall air, crisp with cold, and the ancient stone streets littered with red leaves. The wind that bites ever-so-gently at your cheeks buried in the collar of your jacket. Think of Kyoto, permanently stained red and yellow in your memory: a city on fire. The bitter taste of real green tea on your tongue, the rough stone cup keeping your fingers warm as you huddle together with strangers on a simple wooden bench. The overly sweet candies sitting on a napkin next to you.

The smell.

Japan smells of roses. Dried roses and something else. Something you can't quite put into words. A spice, or maybe just the sea? It's different from America. Older, maybe. Even in Kyoto, one of the biggest cities on the island, everything feels removed from the now. Separate and distant from the modern world, even while watching a car pass in front of you.

Then, just for confusion's sake, there's *yukashii.* Which actually does translate to nostalgic. And more, as is usually the case, including charming, refined, admirable. But what do nostalgic and charming have in common? Can you connect nostalgic and charming, or refined?

Yukashii. A perfect word for Kyoto.

Everything about it screams refined. The way people walk, kimono in every color imaginable with paper umbrellas in hand, a defense against the sun or a sudden rain. The old, so old, impossibly old confectioner shops, still prosperous, opened even before the city was the ancient capital. The maples invading every street and the temples hidden down every alley. The mountains creating a cocoon. It's charming. It's had centuries to define itself and it most definitely has. It lives and breathes in a way you won't find in Tokyo, or Osaka.

Even when you're in the city the place feels nostalgic. I think it's the way Kyoto exists around you, instead of you in Kyoto. It buzzes with activity; aware of itself, of its history. Echoes creep around the city, shading the modern with the past. Think of the imperial palace, a park now - for children to play in, for runners to avoid traffic, for the elderly to take their daily walks. And yet, despite the neon yellow spandex and laughter and giggling, the buildings wait quietly, watching over it all. The gravel crunching under every step, the streets noises muted to whispers. It's hard not to see ghosts in a place so old.

And then you have *shinobu* and *omoiwohaseru*, both meaning to be nostalgic for or think nostalgically of. As verbs, I think they are a little easier to get a feel for. But using them, and actually getting practice with all of this, that's how you're going to learn the language.

The lights up the stairs into the mountains. My favourite place in the whole world. In Fall, the trees catch fire, the clear sound of the temple's waterfall, and the smell of incense carries through the air.

It's packed. The place is full of people crowding against each other, but all I want, my only wish, is to see the sun set from this balcony on my birthday.

The Purple Eyed Opossum of Preston Memorial

James Ebersole

Angela and Charlotte woke up entwined in a tangled mass of sweaty sheets. It was the first properly hot day of Spring, and the open window let in the sound of birdsong and car horns. Angela was the first to wriggle her way out of the linen labyrinth, and therefore on duty to feed the cat and make the morning coffee.

She cradled the resulting hot mug like it was the most precious thing in the world and settled in to their kitchenette table for the half hour left before she had to catch the corner bus to work.

The cat, jealous of the attention Angela was giving to the *Washington Post*, leapt into her lap. In the upset, she barely managed to avoid spilling her coffee on the little beast, and instead doused a front-page photograph of the president, staining his squeeze cheese tan a darker shade.

Before Angela was even able to respond, Charlotte was there at her side, already dabbing up the mess. She was dressed for the day, clad in a floral-hued maternity shirt that, purchased prematurely in the doldrums of a long winter, finally seemed appropriate for the season. Fistful of sopping paper towels, she looked to Angela. "You need to call in sick today," she said.

"What? Why?"

"Call in sick," she repeated, "and pack your things."

They dropped the cat at their elderly neighbor's place, who Charlotte had slyly given notice of the arrangement, with a bottle of chardonnay and a gift card to Panera Bread as payment when the neighbor refused to take cash. After stocking up on sufficient road snacks from the corner store, they loaded their overnight bags into the Prius and drove towards the 14th street bridge.

The cherry blossoms were in bloom; they already knew as much because all the cafes in their rapidly gentrifying neighborhood had themed cocktails, cupcakes, and decorations to fit the occasion. This was their first time seeing the real thing this season. The tourists were out in force, a sea of selfies in a pink, petaled world.

Traffic was heavy going into the district, but the way they were going, opposite of rush hour traffic, was wide open to them. Soon, the suburbs gave way to countryside and mountain views.

Angela spouted out guesses of where they were headed. She began with the likeliest destinations based on geographic proximity, perhaps the Luray Caverns or one of the Virginia vineyards they always promised they'd investigate. But with Charlotte smirking and silent, she got to the point she was saying "Tokyo then. Loch Ness? The International Space Station!" But Charlotte didn't let a clue slip.

Not until they crossed the West Virginia border.

Then, the floodgates opened, and Charlotte excitedly told Angela about everything she had planned for them, describing in great detail the hippy mountain town where you could get forty different flavors of Kombucha, the bed and breakfast with goats and well water on tap, the brewery they simply HAD to visit, even if it would be torture for her not to drink anything.

But they never did the things they planned, and never made it to that bed and breakfast.

They called their child-to-be their little Halloween pumpkin.

That was the due date.

That was what they were promised.

But Charlotte's water broke.

Angela pulled over as soon as she could, stopping the car in the gravelled lot of a scenic outpost overlooking the valley. Everything down there was too tranquil, too vibrant, too green. She wanted to scream at it.

The ambulance was wonderfully responsive, though the five-minute wait still felt unbearably long. The kind and calm EMTs took Charlotte and, with the sirens blaring, were bound for Preston Memorial. Angela followed, driving alone, and quite a bit faster than what she'd normally deem safe for these unfamiliar country roads. Still, she couldn't keep up, and by the time she arrived at the modest regional hospital, she was informed by the help desk receptionist that her wife was already in labor.

She went to the nearest bathroom and threw up the strawberry liquorice and habanero peanuts that had tasted so good in the car, back when everything was in its proper order.

*

She sat in the waiting room, nervous for any update. Others sat there with her, in their own private hells. The temporality of it all felt so askew.

A nurse came into view. He looked pale, nervous, distressed about something. She feared he was coming to tell her some terrible news, but instead, he pulled aside a young orderly, and whispered something. The orderly ran off, and shortly thereafter there was an announcement over the intercom.

"The purple-eyed opossum has broken in to the hospital again. Animal control has been dispatched, and our infection preventionists will work diligently to maintain a safe hospital environment for our patients. I repeat, the purple-eyed visitor is back. If you see her, do not engage. Inform our staff at once."

Some of the others in the waiting room appeared as confused as she was by the announcement. Others seemed to perk up, give each other knowing glances.

Soon, all anyone was talking about was the creature that prowled the hospital. It was a distraction most welcome.

"That creature is the angel of death. Sneaks its way into a room, and bam! Death. I'm not talking just in the hospice ward. Kid comes in with a broken leg from a skateboarding accident, that beast pokes her snout in like she's there to sign the cast, kid gets gangrene and is gone. Just like that."

"That critter ain't sanitary!"

"I hear above the drip, drip of the chemo IV, the pitter patter of her little pale claws against the tile. Maybe she is like a little medusa. One day, I'll set eyes on her, and all the vitality I once had will harden, and I'll be thoroughly metastasized."

"This is what happens when we get socialist Obamacare. Vermin everywhere!"

Angela then added her voice to the mix.

"I think if that opossum shows up here, it's likely to be a good omen. She gives birth to tiny little squirmy things that she carries around. They come out early and grow into being in the outside world."

The waiting room was silent, and they all stared at her like she, in voicing some positive sentiment towards the beast, had simultaneously dropped her pants and uttered the worst string of obscenities imaginable.

"She's a marsupial," Angela added, and this did nothing to help her case.

"My wife just gave birth. Our baby is in intensive care," and this was something they understood, and could empathize with. She expected some sort of homophobic reaction at the mention of a wife, but everyone was immediately consolatory, and it was all kind words of reassurance and comfort.

She started talking, telling them her story, felt like every one of those strangers was a friend she could confide in. It was cathartic.

"How'd you decide who the mother is?" asked the woman who visited weekly to see her coma-bound husband, the most talkative of the lot because she had been coming to the hospital for so very long and knew all the regulars. "Well, you're a mother too, but you get what I'm saying," she added.

The logistics of childbearing with two women always prompted these sorts of innocently offensive (or sometimes downright bizarre) questions, particularly when the inquiring party discovered they were a mixed-race couple. But thankfully, this question had a simple enough answer.

"Because she wanted it more," Angela replied.

*

She went down to the cafeteria under the guise of getting something to eat, but really, she needed to stretch her legs, to engage herself in the simple pleasure of a human body not currently in need of treatment.

There was a weird vibe to the place. She noticed anytime anyone went to throw something away they did it sheepishly, and at a distance, trying not to get too close to the bin lest the opossum spring out from the rubbish. One woman in the corner eyed her salad suspiciously, as if some strange and tiny monster would scurry out from beneath the thickest chunk of iceberg lettuce.

Angela bought a single bulbous red apple, the skin of it waxy, feeling fake. The cashier did the transaction with a single hand, the other tightly clutching a push broom, perhaps to sweep away the fugitive marsupial in the event it decided to come around and steal some food.

She went back up to the waiting room, apple in hand, steeling herself for whatever conversation would greet her.

But the entire area, bustling with activity only moments ago, was completely empty. She sat, and bit into the apple in silence, the crunch of it echoing through the empty and sterile space.

She heard something shift among the scattered magazines piled on the corner table. She looked and saw the very animal that had taken on a mythic quality over the past hour.

Its eyes were two shining beacons positioned above a sneering snout, teeth bared. The amethyst glow reflected back at her, seemed to be reaching into her soul.

She held out the apple, the juice from the single bite she had taken dripping down her hand. The creature's nostrils twitched in reply. Angela rested the apple on cover of the closest magazine to her reach, *Time Magazine*, the person of the year issue dedicated to the silence breakers of the #MeToo movement. Her hand was so close to the creature she could feel its hot breath.

The opossum, after determining Angela was no threat, lunged for the apple and scurried away. In the movement, for the briefest moment, Angela thought she could see a tiny squirming pink babe in the animal's pouch.

Soon, the waiting room began to fill up again, and all signs that the purple eyed visitor had been there vanished.

Angela tried to sleep curled up on a chair; she thought of their cat back home, and how easily that little weasel could sleep anywhere, but it was no use. Sleep would not come. A piece of apple had wedged itself between two molars, and she incessantly prodded the fibers of it with her tongue. She was certain that this, and this alone, was keeping her awake, and only if she could dislodge it she could sleep soundly and without worry or grief.

In the early morning, Angela and Charlotte were led to a quiet room, with couches that looked so fluffy and plump that, had they been in the waiting room the prior night, she may have fallen into one and never woken up.

Soft piano music played somewhere in the corner of the room. Angela thought she could hear tiny claws against the linoleum, but perhaps it was only static on the speakers.

The neonatal clinician came in and told them the news, in what was surely a nuanced performance of a finely tuned script, with improvisation tailored to their particular grief. But Angela wasn't paying attention. She was staring out the window and down into the parking lot, where animal control was loading their caged and leering captive into the van.

*

After being discharged, the couple drove back to D.C. in silence. Though the sky was choked with the threat of rain, they both wore sunglasses. Angela as a safeguard against the intermittent and blinding bursts of sun, and Charlotte for perhaps the same reason, or as a sort of plastic funerary veil for bloodshot eyes vacantly staring at their own reflection in the lens.

Angela was driving on autopilot, lost in her head, a head that was thinking nothing but swimming in the approximate motions of thought.

"Pull over here," Charlotte requested, breaking the silence.

Angela stopped the car at the observation point, one not too dissimilar to the one where they called the ambulance.

Charlotte got out of the car, and Angela followed.

When they first left the air-conditioned hospital, the heat and humidity smothered them, but up there the air was cool, a breeze stirring specks of pollen over everything.

Charlotte pointed down into the trees below.

"That's where the child lives now," she whispered.

Angela pulled Charlotte close, resting her chin on her shoulder, breathing her in.

Hospital grade soap could not mask her beautiful scent. They held each other so tight, watching the clouds drift over the valley.

When Angela finally let go and started back for the car, she noticed the oddest thing at the very precipice of the watch point. Where the railing ended there was a bench, positioned hazardously close to the edge. Above the bench was a lamppost inexplicably placed at the very edge of the drop off. The dirt had loosened where the post was planted. It seemed to lean into the valley, looking as though it would topple and go crashing down at any moment. The glass had been shattered, and where the bulb should have been there was a tangled orb of branches and feathers, a bird's nest in the most impossible and precarious of places.

Angela started laughing, and caught herself, afraid that such an ill-suited reaction would be inappropriate for the moment. But Charlotte only softly smiled back.

Back on the road, the image of the bird's nest at the watch point remained in Angela's mind. It reminded her of one on the porch of her childhood home. The nest had been there for years and sat dormant for as long as she could remember. Then, one day, another nest sprouted beside it. She didn't know why any bird would think it was a good idea to build something new right next to the abandoned ruins of another nest.

But the older she got, the more such a thing made sense.

Movement in the roadside gully broke her reverie; with the movement were two purple glowing orbs that were gone just as she sees them. It was at that exact same moment they were crossing state lines, truly heading home, to a quiet apartment, to malnourished houseplants and the forgotten potatoes, sprouting and spongey, the beer cans left in the recycling smelling sticky sweet, home to what felt like a restart, or a new beginning altogether.

She reached across the center console for her wife's hand, startled to find a tiny marsupial paw reaching back.

#NoBadVibes

Katy Lennon

First Published in Shoreline of Infinity, Issue 11 for International Woman's Day March 2018.

CASE STUDY NO. 89 – LOCAL TERRA YEAR: 2020

[BEGIN AUDIO TRANSCRIPT – ARTICLE TWO]

Hey what's up you guys, it's Pixie! And I'm back with a follow-up video that I never thought I'd make! [LAUGH]

For those of you who haven't seen my original unboxing video, I've linked it in the description box, so please go check it out! So, shit's been going *down*! If you follow me you'll already know all about it, but I just want to address a few things in this video. For those of you who were concerned for my safety, don't worry! I got rid of all the gross, weird stuff they sent me. It's all in the garbage, where it belongs! [LAUGH]

[EDITOR'S NOTE: A full breakdown of the items gifted to the terrestrials in this particular instance is available at personal request. Original transcript file is indefinitely unavailable.]

You guys had a massive response, my tweet about it even started a trending hashtag, #Justice4Pixie, that was pretty crazy! And listen, I know that everything you guys do comes from a place of love, and shows how much you care about me, and that makes me feel so good because I love you all so much!

But, you know you have to look after yourselves. I heard about a few of you turning up to the alien base, and I know it was just to talk about the box they sent me, but you WILL get vaporized! Too many of you guys have been already, and I just can't condone that! I know you just love me and care about me, but you have to be careful!

And I know a lot of you wanted me to address the death threats? That the aliens claim to be receiving? I highly doubt that any of you guys would do that, so I think there might be a bit of embellishing happening there. I know all of you so well, and I just don't think it's in any of your natures to say something like that.

[EDITOR'S NOTE: In this particular instance, the terrestrial selected for contact maintained a following of over 10 million other beings on her home planet. In this case, individual specie traits such as pride and self-image were not acknowledged. Since then, extensive research is done before establishing contact, making each one adaptive to the life forms in question.]

But maybe they're like, misunderstanding you or something, so I think its best you don't communicate at all.

Okay, I have a feeling I'll be making another update video about this pretty soon! [LAUGH] so I'm not gonna say that is the end of this! Let's just say they've been in touch, and I think we've found a way to resolve the issue. Don't forget to like, comment and subscribe, thank you guys so so much for watching and I'll see you next time! Bye!

[END AUDIO TRANSCRIPT – ARTICLE TWO]

[BEGIN AUDIO TRANSCRIPT – ARTICLE THREE]

Hey you guys, it's Pixie. So, I'm feeling pretty pissed off that I even have to make this video. It's a complete joke and, like I honestly can't believe we're being treated this way. I've already posted on my daily story about this but it pissed me off so much I had to sit down and talk to you about it. So, like I mentioned in the update video, I have been in touch with the alien occupiers, but things have not gone as well as I thought they might.

I thought they would apologize for sending me that gross box, and maybe show me some cool alien shit, like let me see into the future or something. They always seem nicer in the movies, even if they mostly ended up blowing us up. I always thought they seemed cool. But they were not like that AT ALL. I turned up to the base and... well there was a lot to deal with. For one thing, they were ugly af! [LAUGH] I thought they might be cute, like little green dudes, but no! Pot-bellied weirdos, all of them! And they were all NAKED! That was pretty distracting, straight off the bat.

THEN! They didn't even want to apologize?! And honestly? I kinda tuned out after they refused to say sorry, that was the whole reason I'd gone all the way over there. They kept going on about using me as a 'beacon' to 'spread their message' to the people of Earth. But I wasn't really listening. Actually, I got to burn them pretty good, I waited until they'd said their whole spiel, then I just looked at them totally deadpan and was like 'So, you're saying this has been a total waste of my time?'

> [EDITOR'S NOTE: This response was key in ending the debate in favour of planet liquidation. It is important to consider local colloquialisms when determining a planet's fate. These testimonies can be downloaded on personal request.]

It was so great, I totally owned them! [LAUGH]

They even asked me about that thing in the bottle, do you guys remember that? I told them I found it slithering about my room like a creep and I got my bf to kill it with a shoe. Oh man, they were not happy about that.

> [EDITOR'S NOTE: All visiting life forms involved in cautionary missions are now protected under the Life Form as Commodity Law]

Apparently, it was this magic creature that could have cured world hunger or something? Like it shits plants that we can eat? I was like who wants to eat a shit plant though? [LAUGH] That thing was GROSS I wasn't about to keep it in my house!

Anyways, they kept going on and on at me, getting more and more dramatic, saying the 'fate of the planet was in my hands', humanity is 'on a path to destruction', just clickbaity shit like that. They kept asking me to tell everyone to 'change their ways or face obliteration,' I was like, um I don't have that kind of influence, I only just got verified on Twitter. Plus, fuck you pay me, bitch! [LAUGH] Apparently the whole box thing was their way of connecting with me, to try and get me to spread this message. Um, I think they need new PR staff, tbh! Because that was a hot mess.

> [EDITOR'S NOTE: The Visual Warning Law prevented the use of this method, and required all cautionary expeditions to include visual aids as part of their campaigns.]

I just wanted to get out of there ASAP, so when they asked me for my final answer I was like 'Bitch, I already told you! NO!' [LAUGH] After that they FINALLY let me leave. Pretty soon after that, their nasty looking spaceship flew away. I don't even know why, they're so fucking petty.

Everyone In my comments section seems pretty concerned about it, but I don't think we have anything to worry about. We're, like, the best planet in the solar system! Let them go back where they came from, our cultures are obviously just not compatible. For all you haters saying we're about to be annihilated, STFU and get off my page! #NoBadVibes!

Hopefully that should be the last video I make about this whole thing! Thank fuck it's all over with! We can finally get back to the things that really matter. I'll have a new haul for you guys next week! Don't forget to like, comment and subscribe, I love you guys so so much, and I will see you next time! Bye!

[END AUDIO TRANSCRIPT – ARTICLE THREE]

END

Name Day

G.M. Barbour

The morning is bright, too bright for such an early hour. Sunlight slices into the living room, heating the clothes-covered sofa, revealing every smudge and smear on the coffee table. The husband stands in the kitchen, ignoring last night's dirty dishes while sipping tea cooling beyond the point of perfection. On the table sits a baby bag stuffed with blankets, nappies and everything else he's remembered to pack.

Upstairs in the bathroom, the wife shrugs on mismatched clothes. A feeding top and jogger bottoms. They're the only things clean that fit. Slipping on her shoes, she regards her reflection in the mirror above the sink. Scrapes her hair from her face. Contemplates the lines around her eyes and the fullness of her figure. She thinks about putting on face cream, perhaps some mascara, when the baby starts to cry and her

breasts ache. "Darling, could you get her?" she calls to the husband, taking her face cream from the bathroom cabinet and popping the lid.

"What's that?" he shouts from downstairs.

"Never mind," she mutters, dropping the cream back on the shelf. She shuts the cabinet door with more firmness than necessary.

The bedroom is dark and warm with the unmistakable aroma of fabric softener and milk. She opens the curtains, letting the light in, and baby cries louder, her screams angry and urgent. The wife picks up her daughter, who makes small grunts as she detects that familiar smell. The wife rests back on the double bed, readying to feed. Although she's got the hang of it now, she's still worried she's not doing it right. It nips a bit, and it was hard, so hard before, she almost gave up. She may yet…

Baby drinks happily, not wasting a drop. That feeling, questioning whether she's doing the right thing, will it ever go away?

"All okay?" The husband asks, popping his head round the door.

"Yes." The wife waves a hand and the husband is meant to understand. "I mean, no. But yes."

After a moment, with cotton wool softness, he asks, "The name?"

She nods. The back of her throat tightens and she gulps, squeezing her lips tight. It's no use. Hot tears drip down her cheeks, splashing onto her top and seeping through the fabric. It's silly really, she knows this. She shouldn't be so upset, it's not uncommon. Lots of people have trouble naming their babies. Her cousin went without a name for as long as was possible and her niece was named after a midwife. Still. They should have come up with something by now. But every time they have an idea one of them hates it. Or it reminds them of someone they don't like. Worse, their friends' children are called something similar. And, well, family names just don't fit. Not for their daughter, who's so special, unique, and deserving of a name that embodies her exceptional entrance to this world. It has to be perfect. After everything she's been through in her short life, she's worthy of a name synonymous with strength and resilience, but also peace and love and-

"Sweetheart," he says, dropping to his knees so he's almost level with her. Who knew his eyebrows could raise so high? "It's okay."

"It's not though!" She squeaks, annoyed at how pathetic she sounds. "I don't want it to be like this. I don't want us to be those people."

"What people? What do you mean?"

"People who don't name their child on the sodding birth certificate!"

The baby stops drinking and gives a sharp moan. Husband and wife share a glance, and while mother burps daughter, they continue in calmer tones.

"We don't have to leave it blank," the husband says, knees cracking as he stands and stretches. He yawns, eyeing up the space on the bed beside his wife.

"Sorry?"

He sees the look on her face and gulps. "If you're worried. About it being blank."

The wife's brows draw together and a crease appears above her nose. "You're suggesting… what?"

"Well, uh, just pop down any old thing and we can change it later."

Her frown unfolds into wide-eyed horror. " 'Any. Old. Thing'?"

He runs a hand down his face, closing his eyelids with his fingertips. With a sigh, he opens them and meets her gaze, pouring all his love into his smile. "If you'd prefer it to a blank space, yes."

The silence that falls between them is popped by a tiny burp. Husband and wife chuckle despite themselves, their attention drawn to the little human who is their world.

"Sweetheart…"

The wife looks up and sees her husband edging closer to the bedroom door. "Yes, darling?"

Pause. "We have to go."

She knows he's right, of course he is. Yet she remains on the bed, holding her daughter close. Baby's eyes are open, bleary and sparkly as only new-borns' are. Amid the chaos, trauma, the hazy time between going into labour and when they finally brought their daughter home, the wife has known how to draw strength. This. The closeness. The safeness of home.

"Sweetheart," he presses.

Unable to face him, she stares at the heap of unwashed clothes in the corner of the room. Somewhere downstairs her phone buzzes with yet another message she's no intention of answering. Her body tenses as the prospect of leaving the house fizzes in her chest and she chews at her already bitten raw nails.

The husband bends over and places his hand on her shoulder. The warmth and weight spread through her muscles, pressing her downwards. She shakes him off.

"Please-"

"You're too heavy!"

"No! Look." He takes a deep breath and stands upright. "I know you're upset but we have to go." His voice is firm. Insistent. "We're already late. Please."

He holds his arms out for his daughter. The wife gives him a look that speaks her mind. Nevertheless, she knows he's right, and with a sigh she hands him the baby. Swinging her legs off the bed, she stands and gives herself a shake.

"Fine," she says. "But I'm putting on face cream before we leave."

He doesn't argue, too busy holding his daughter, head bowed, eyes moist. The wife watches, notes the swell in her chest and captures the moment, a snapshot for the memory banks. As he continues to linger, gently rocking the baby, the wife gives him instructions for getting ready to depart. He can't do anything without being told, it seems.

The cream is cool and seeps into her skin. The fresh yet gentle scent enlivens the process, making feel luxurious. A treat. She rubs hard, pushing the stretched, whirling sensation from her forehead. She ignores her reflection, looking instead through the textured glass at the fluttering, sun spilled leaves. The creeping fears which threaten to rise up her throat are swallowed down in long breaths. What will come, will come. Unbothered by the greasy marks she'll leave, she presses her fingers against the window pane. It's warm.

Returning the cream to the cabinet, she closes the door shut with a click. Taking one last steadying breath, she returns to her room to fetch her sunglasses before heading downstairs.

Ten minutes later, they're pulling out the tight driveway in their reliable little car. Sunshine blares though every window. Their daughter rests in front, car seat strapped in, facing backwards. The passenger seat airbag has been disengaged since the day they'd left the hospital. The wife needs to be able to reach her daughter easily. And the husband knows his wife needs their daughter close. He won't argue over where the baby seat should go. He sits in the back, an arm looped through the straps of the bulging baby bag. The radio is switched to a station that dabbles in songs from days gone by. They journey without talking, enjoying the music, until they hear an unmistakable opening riff. One of their songs.

The wife gasps, bouncing a little, desperate to see her husband in the rear view mirror. She can't, but feels his hand on her shoulder. Unlike before, the weight is perfect and heat spreads through her like an embrace. The lyrics kick-in and they sing. His voice vibrates through his fingers, she'd swear it. They're not perfectly in tune, but together they harmonise and follow the melody without missing a word or beat. All the while the baby's silent, half asleep, lulled by a full belly and the surrounding rhapsody.

They arrive at the registrar, find a space to park, but remain in their car until the end of the song. As it concludes, the wife switches the radio off, refusing the presenter a chance spoil the moment with inane, chipper chatter. Thick silence fills the air.

After a moment, she turns and asks, "You remember?"

"Yes," he replies. One word speaks a thousand more.

It seemed utterly crazy they hadn't considered it before. The lists, late night internet searches, endless suggestions from family, and the constant flicking through waiting room magazines for inspiration. All the while, the answer had been available at the push of a button.

"We always said -"

"Yes!"

She pauses, unsure, bubbling at the prospect of striking gold. "So you're thinking what I'm thinking?"

"Yes," he answers, and he's never sounded so certain about anything. "It's perfect."

The wife gives a small cry and brings her hands to her mouth. A faint, high-pitched sound escapes her as she comprehends what's happened. Without another word, she springs out the car and opens the boot.

They unload, pop the baby in the pram and, only forty-five minutes late, check-in for their appointment. In the bare waiting area they sit for hardly a minute before a woman in a navy suit calls their surname. The husband slings the baby bag over his shoulder, while his wife pushes the pram, and they follow the woman down a sunlit corridor.

"Lovely morning!" the registrar breezes as she ushers them into the stark little office. She stops to bend over the pram. "Hello there!" she says wiggling her many-ringed fingers. "Aren't you adorable?"

She settles into the seat behind her desk and taps her computer to life.

"So sorry we're late," the wife says, plopping into one of the two chairs opposite.

The husband sits next to her, resting the bag on the floor.

The registrar waves a hand. "Everyone's late for these, don't worry. Right." She turns from her screen and smiles at them both. "Have we got a name for the wee one?"

Taking deep breaths, husband and wife glance at each other, smile, and nod. The reach out and clasp each other's hand. Then, at the same time, they say their daughter's name.

The Merry Dancers

By Helen-Anne Ross

"I'm sorry, Miss MacLeod, it's not good news."

I was afraid of that, Doctor. How long have I got?"

"About six months, maybe a year."

Dora had long known the cancer was back. Told the nice doctor she'd have palliative care if it got painful. Otherwise no drugs, no chemo, quite sure thank you, just let it take its course and gather ye rosebuds while ye may. She said.

Later she stared through her window at a blackbird pecking at crumbs thrown onto her frosted lawn. Who would miss her? A few good friends, dwindling in number. The Grim Reaper scything merrily away. She contemplated a small, silver zinc bucket on the windowsill containing a cactus in a pot - it was supposed to flower but never had. Lifting the pot, she fumbled underneath for the grubby piece of paper with its scrawled list.

Two weeks later she was cruising to Tromsø, having cashed her supplementary pension. Number one on the bucket list had been seeing the Aurora Borealis, and the forecast was good. That was the way to go - no hanging around suffering pain and disability, a burden to random others. She'd wait until the Lights came, leave an explanatory farewell note in the cabin, jump over the side into Artic water and expire in an explosion of green light. She'd be drowned and dead of hypothermia in 10 minutes, and there would be no body for some poor friend or council employee to discover. Perhaps a polar bear would recycle her.

The first two nights she slept like an infant, gently lulled by the soft burr of the ship's motor, northward bound. In the daytime, she leaned over the deck rail meditatively observing the swell of the ocean and planning her escape. Into the great sleep awaiting her. She wondered if she had ever really been awake. Events seeming to hold such import for other people's lives had passed her by. There had been no marriage, no children, no passionate consuming career, just a humdrum office job with now and again a trip to Torremolinos in the summer holidays. She'd dutifully looked after her parents when they were very old, and that had taken up quite a bit of time and energy. And money. They had both said they wished they could just jump off a cliff and she had hushed them in shock. But they were right, perhaps she'd get to tell them so. Who knew?

At meal times she gazed at the elderly cruisers gorging on mountains of perfectly presented food, but could hardly take more than a morsel herself. When they went ashore to consume hot chocolate and cream in the cafes of tiny snow-bound towns, she remained in her room. Most were couples sitting in silence in the evenings, nursing their liqueurs as musicians determined to earn a living tried to create an atmosphere. They clung to each other and their prejudices like limpets and they thought her odd. She spent time composing a farewell note. To whom?

On the third day, she retired to her cabin after a stilted and frugal supper in the company of German widows. She was lying in her bed when a shout went up in various languages – "The Lights!" She put on her coat over her pyjamas and left the note neatly centred on the bedspread. Once on the higher deck facing the ocean, tiny tear icicles pulled down her lower eyelids. Green lights glowed and flashed all around the heavens to excited Oohs and Aahs. Too many people. She stole to a deserted spot on the coast side deck, climbed the rail as quickly as her stiffened limbs would allow and jumped. With a crunch she fell heavily into a lifeboat on the deck below, her leg twisted and awry beneath her.

Dizzy with pain, Dora lay staring at the swirling lights twinkling and modulating from green to yellow. They seemed to dance against the horizon. All at once, a great, shimmering, translucent shape swished across the heavens scattering the dancing effervescence. It looked like an enormous Arctic Fox, its great brush sweeping the hilltops beyond the fjords over the coastline and out onto the sea. Finding her, it reared up then presented its brush. Its eyes were diamond hard and piercing although not unkind, They challenged her. What could she do but rise and mount its back? The pain vanished as she rode upon the Fox through the sky, which now flashed green and red and yellow as they coursed the frosted, sparkling heavens. Misty, dancing beings with starry headdresses twirled around them. Sounds of an unearthly sweetness resonated in her ears, music to listen to for an eternity. "Follow, follow, dance with us", they sang, "upon the frozen wastes we await you. Awake and come with us our precious one, our queen awaits you!" There below were vast plains of shimmering ice. The Fox made a softly padding landing and lay down to let her slip from its back. Before her the dancers circled in a roundelay. Dora heard a gentle laughter rippling through the music and her heart felt an ecstasy unbeknown to her until now. All the elements of existence were no more than the tiny glass pieces in a child's kaleidoscope, shifting and reforming into the most beautiful of patterns. She whirled and reeled within the roundel of dancers, as the music swelled and quickened. Until it climaxed and died and the dancers sank into profound bows and curtseys. In a flash the dance shape opened out and Dora saw advancing towards her a glittering throng. Goodness me that must be the queen, she's a sight for sore eyes, she thought. That's a pretty glitzy crowd with her. Behind them many figures stood before citadels of ice, carved and glistening in the lights.

"Who have you brought me, Master Fox?" inquired the splendid figure, gesturing with a silver sceptre that sparkled and flickered. The Fox nudged Dora with its tail, so she approached the Lady. The closer she came, the more she felt an immense love envelope her. How extraordinary, why would someone love me like this? We haven't been even introduced!

But she found herself whispering, murmuring all that she was, had wished she were and would become. A torrent of words flowed towards the beautiful Lady who listened so patiently. Dora felt acceptance, compassion and love encircle her, rosy, glowing. She sank to her knees surrounded by the courtly retinue as the Lady raised the silver sceptre. Lightning flashes seared the heavens and Dora jolted as one bolt felled her. She lost consciousness.

When at last she revived, the Fox was observing her kindly. And no one else, they were alone upon the vast wastes of untrodden snow. The music had faded and the lights were gone. It told her it was time to return. Raising her onto its back, it covered her gently with its brush and hurtled towards the ship.

"Who were they and who are you?" breathed Dora in its ear.

"I am Revuntulet, the Great Snow Fox. You have seen the Merry Dancers and their Queen, dear one. But it is not your time. Now you must return to your life and not forget us. You have been asleep and now your eyes are open. Know that we are always there, dancing, in spite of what most people think! The moon still exists when the sun shines, does it not? Moonlight reflects the light of the hidden sun."

Later, Dora heard she had nearly died of pneumonia. Lying in pyjamas with a broken leg all night in the Arctic air will do that to you. After her airlift from the ship, she passed a most satisfactory time in a Norwegian hospital. Researching the Internet between physiotherapy appointments, surprisingly tasty hospital meals and excellent care. The nurses spoke such good English! She read of the Merry Dancers, the Hebridean name for the Northern Lights. And of the Snow Fox whom Estonians believed roamed the heavens. She returned to Glasgow a happier woman – and to her surprise and delight the cactus had produced a flower!

She joined a Gaelic choir and even started learning the language. Her broken leg was scarcely a trouble and, once fully mobile, she enrolled in a country-dancing class for exercise and traditional, homespun fun. The memory of the dancers, the queen and their love slowly faded. She did wonder what was all that about, now and again. She grieved a little for her great snow fox and what he'd showed her. Although ordinary things were now far more interesting and enjoyable, they really were. Maybe it was enough just to be happy, life had certainly become much more agreeable. People were a lot friendlier and nicer to her now she was more appreciative of them.

Next time she saw the consultant he told her the cancer hadn't progressed, tumour the same size, what have you been doing, Miss MacLeod? Whatever it is, for Goodness sake go on doing it! And you look so well too! She almost skipped out of the Polyclinic and didn't care who saw her.

That autumn, she went to the Isle of Skye with her Gaelic choir, hoping to find a bit of merriment and some native speakers. There weren't many around, but she eventually found one – at a ceilidh in Portree. They got chatting in the vestibule as, kilted in red tartan, he helped her shed her sodden coat. His name was Rory Fuchs and he joked in Gaelic with the tea ladies about their gigantic dented aluminium teapots. He had a mane of snow-white hair, a melodious voice and his toes seemed to twinkle as he slipped them into his soft black leather dancing shoes. Mercy me what's going on with his toes, she thought. His eyes twinkled too, frosty blue and kind. So she said yes to his gallant invitation to the Eightsome Reel, the first of an exhausting range of dances. No one else asked her, no one else got the chance, he'd taken possession of her, really he had. When they were out of puff, it was sitting and talking, what a relief no more bouncing around pretending you were in the first flush of youth. She'd been feeling more tired again recently, a bit worrying, just a niggle. But she really couldn't remember when she had got on so well with a man to tell the truth, certainly none had ever made her almost split her sides laughing. He was from the far North, but visited Glasgow often. She let the others return to the hotel, they could manage fine without her. She could also do without the winks and elbow nudges some were already making.

After the last waltz had come and gone, Rory asked if he could escort her back to the hotel. He suggested a stroll along the waters edge in spite of the chill. His eyes sparkled keenly in the silvery moonshine as the waves lapped the pebbly shore and a faint scent of seaweed wafted up the sea loch.

"You know, you can see the Northern Lights from here, I saw them this last winter."

"So did I!" said Dora, "In Norway, a trip cruising in the Arctic. I was so excited I fell over the side into a lifeboat, broke my leg and got pneumonia. So stupid of me. It will have been a fever hallucination of course, but I really did fancy I was in among the Merry Dancers, dancing for my life!"

He turned away and went to sit upon a rock. The moon emerged from behind a tiny cloud and shone bright and strong. She could see him shimmer in its radiance. Yet he was warmer and more solid than anything she had ever known.

"Ah me dear, perhaps you were. The mysteries of our dreams and the purpose of our fancies, indeed of our lives, are aye present. Their shape is often strangely shrouded – and sometimes clouds obscure them, sometimes we are determined to look elsewhere. But the dancers are always dancing, even behind the light of day. You just have to pay attention."

"Oh", said Dora.

He smiled, and his teeth glistened in the moonlight. It struck her how large they were, she hadn't noticed that before. How interesting. Then he held out his hand.

"Come, we shall be very good friends, you and I. Don't you think?"

She smiled back at him as they walked forward, wading hand in hand into the freezing water. Had she ever felt so happy, in spite of the pebbles sharp beneath her soles and the chill creeping upwards until tiny waves lapped against her chin? She thought not. She raised her gaze to the North where a flash of green trembled above the horizon.

It was time.

Transformations

Danusia Staunton

The trees are coming into leaf, like something almost being said. I suppose I've always rather liked that line of Larkin's, even though it's patent nonsense. Like something *almost* said? After all, that's something *not* said, in the end. And trees do indeed bud and grow leaves. I guess I would probably agree that spring isn't the loudest season, though. If anything, it's autumn. No coy whisperings from autumn. She veritably yells, dumping those all-too-soon-browned leaves about the place without a by-your-leave. And then she rains all over everything, leaving that brown, once leafy mush for us all to slip on. Yes. Autumn is the loudest season. She's just ghastly.

It was the great oak outside Holborn station that had incited Jenny's impotent rage against the shifting tides of the year. It shone a brilliant red, boasting that beautiful moment before the outward withering of winter. Even if April *is* the cruellest month, she pondered on in literary resentment, November's got to be plain angry.

She left the station, bracing her collar against the wind, and turned down Newton Street. It was there she'd arranged to pick up the car. Stuart had been kind to lend it to her for the weekend, even if it did smell of stale cigarettes and had suspicious stains on the upholstery. As soon as she turned the corner, Jenny could see it parked up the street. It seemed somehow more rusty than she remembered and she hoped it would hold out. But beggars can't be choosers, she thought.

She got in, started up the unwilling engine and pulled away from the kerb. It had been far too long and she felt twitchy in the traffic. Eye out for speed traps and taking wary note of busses, she made her way from the bustling epicentre of the city, past high-rise blocks, grotty looking takeaways, dilapidated warehouses and seemingly endless traffic lights. As the centre began to melt into suburbs, from the bird's eye view of the Hammersmith flyover she saw the old brewery and wondered if it was still in use. Past schools and cemeteries she drove, feeling more comfortable now she'd adjusted to it, less worried about errant cabbies or wayward London pedestrians bustling their way so arrogantly, or was it absent-mindedly, into the road.

Onwards she drove, outwards from the city. Roads widening, there were fewer people now. She relaxed into it, despite her destination, and almost began enjoying herself. By the time she reached the country lanes, she had forgotten the purpose of all this, this revisiting of the past that had been so unceremoniously thrust upon her by her nearest and dearest. And somehow, now, in the endless countryside, she felt less annoyed by this enforced exodus. Being called away from the city almost felt like a relief. Like something almost being said.

Turning into the driveway of the old place felt strange. Not far from here had been where she'd failed her first driving test. Not far from here had been where she and David had fallen into that ditch in the darkness as they stumbled home from the pub. There was the bus stop where James had held her hand. How it flooded back, she thought, though her own sentimentality had taken her unawares and had irritated her. And here was the old house, somewhat greyer than before, though neat still.

Walking up the stone steps, she heard a dim familiar calling from the kitchen and inhaled deeply the warm familiar smell. As the last clutches of irritation slipped away, she rang the doorbell and realised, she felt at home.

VOICE OF REASON

Alexandra Balasa

Orkaedis Durant had always known that mental strength was the key to acquiring immunity from the epidemic known as the 'Voices.' If the Voices were parasites that used emotion to enter victims' minds, if they fed on thoughts, then they'd be thwarted if victims withheld all thoughts and emotions from them. Surely, with enough training, people could learn to erect mental walls.

It was this passion to prove himself, to cure the Voice epidemic, that led him to reject his heritage. Who would take an irrigation farmer of the Akkutian desert seriously? That background wasn't suitable for one of the Vangardian Empire's leading mental practitioners. Upon immigrating he adopted the Vangardian spelling of *Orcadis*, and labored to rid himself of his Akkutian accent with its harsh 'k' and 'r' inflections. He succeeded because unlike most, he knew all limitations were mental. That knowledge had long unchained his own mind, turned him from an impoverished desert laborer into a head researcher in Vangarde.

His wife had been amused when he'd founded the mental fortification organization he called the Iron Helms. "What good are gurus and monks against an epidemic like this?" she'd asked. "We don't know anything about the Voices. Why they can't get through physical barriers, how they use emotion to attach to minds, what they *are*."

Negativity: another mental barrier that had never applied to Orcadis. So, with his golden hair and bronze skin and perfect teeth lending credibility to his ambition, he accrued a following. At the beginning he personally trained each new initiate. Pain desensitization and meditation and projection and a dozen other mental feats of his invention. He sneered at the terms 'monk' and 'guru.' The Helms were warriors. They adorned their robes with chainmail and wore silver coronets to symbolize mental constraint.

After some years, his wife began using words like "cold" and "negligent." For how long could she entertain his delusion? He'd turned ambition into obsession. With all his 'desensitization training', he'd alienated her and their young son. Those words, after all the Akkutian lore Orcadis had related to his family? Tales of heroes among sand dunes who had their families' unwavering support? A spouse wasn't supposed to say, "Stop trying to save the world and pay attention to me." And though he tried to express his affection as before, his fingers were stiff caressing his wife's cheek, his baritone flat when he told his boy stories he'd once recited with animation.

When she left, taking her self-imposed limitations with her, Orcadis was a little relieved. As mindful as he'd always been, it took that relief to realize his Helm training had let him transcend emotion. He'd entered the realm of detachment. Any remaining threads of attachment snapped when she tried to take their son. Years together must not have taught her that Orcadis rivalled the Voices in how well he knew minds. It wasn't as if he didn't try to warn her. He was detached, not cruel. She laughed when Orcadis said he could convince the High King's representatives she was an unsuitable parent. A few months later, Vangarde's Royal Court granted him guardianship of Orcadis Junior.

The boy started calling himself Kaed after that. *Kaed* – the section Orcadis had cut from his name so many years ago. It was a blatant and dramatic rejection of everything his father was. That gesture would have wounded Orkaedis the irrigation farmer, and even Orcadis the budding mental practitioner. But not Greathelm Orcadis Durant. Greathelm Orcadis understood that children go through phases after their parents' separation. 'Kaed' would act out his drama and return to good sense. Besides, it was bad conditioning to reward behavior problems with attention. Orcadis paid no heed. Like the heroes from the lore he'd shared with his son what seemed a lifetime ago, he turned his gaze to the common good and focused on training his Iron Helms.

By building their minds, the Iron Helms did gain immunity to the Voices. Orcadis was first. One day, like a path-forging prophet, he went out into the thick of a Swarm. He moved against the masses shrieking and scrambling to get indoors. How ridiculous they were, covering their ears and shaking their heads like crazed bulls trying to dislodge riders. The streets cleared and he remained unmoved. People watched him from windows with the morbid fascination that lured crowds to executions. And an execution it must be; nobody could resist more than five minutes in a Swarm without getting Infected. And yet, half an hour later, the Swarm had passed and Orcadis's mind was unscathed. Lies, everyone said. Within a few weeks, he would lose himself as the mental parasite inhabiting his brain fed off his thoughts. First, he'd start talking to himself. Then the Voice in his head would become more real to him than anything. He'd withdraw from society and forget how to speak, how to function. Eventually he would lapse into catatonia, a husk, his mind drained of thoughts. And the blood-sucker in his brain, grown stronger with Orcadis's energy, would move on in search of a new host.

The months passed and Orcadis's mind remained unmarred. The Iron Helms received royal patronage that next year. Their numbers rose from a few dozen to over two thousand initiates. Orcadis asked his son if he'd been afraid, if like the others he'd doubted his father's claims. The boy admitted to feeling more resignation than anything. "There's no real way to lose you," he'd said. "I never had you in the first place. You might not have gotten Infected, Father, but the Voices have you. They've always had you."

It was the kind of negativity that made Orcadis accept the appropriateness of Kaed's name change. He started using the new name after that, though whenever he said *Kaed*, his stomach clenched in the closest approximation to pain he was capable of feeling since desensitization training.

#

Kaed couldn't remember his first encounter with the Voices. Their existence had been so prevalent in his life that he confused memories with stories other Helms told his father, and stories his father told him. Once, he'd bragged to friends about fending off an entire Swarm by clearing his mind and disembodying his consciousness. He'd barely gotten to the part about lifting out of his body when a classmate had interrupted to say he'd had the same experience a week prior. Because one didn't just outright call the Greathelm's son a liar.

It was Orcadis who'd informed Kaed of his real first experience with the Voices. He'd been five years old, and back then, Vangarde and its colonies had still been figuring out how to predict Swarms. The curfews and the Emergency Accommodation acts hadn't been established, much less the beacons that warned of a Swarm's arrival up to forty minutes in advance. Back then, Swarms were uncommon and unpredictable, and on that day, one swept through the city unannounced.

Kaed had been picnicking with his parents at a park when a buzz grew audible on the horizon, like an approaching cloud of locusts. Within moments that sound grew to a thunderous roar, thousands of Voices whispering, competing for entrance into vulnerable brains. People began falling to their knees, clutching their heads as the wave passed over them. Orcadis, more adept at resisting the Voices than anyone, scooped Kaed up with one arm, seized his wife's hand with the other, and found shelter. Some minutes later, safe in an alehouse across the street, Kaed had pulled on his father's sleeve.

"Daddy," he'd said, barely audible over the screams and the Voices thickening the air outside. "I've made so many new friends."

And he'd smiled. Orcadis liked to tell that story as the prime example of everything that was wrong with his son. "We are mental warriors, Kaed," he'd say. "Our minds are fortresses, and our enemies are at the gates. They come waving white flags and spouting promises of truce, of alliance, but we mustn't let them in. If we do, they will raze our cities to the ground."

It was a miracle Kaed hadn't gotten Infected then. He often wondered what the Voices told him that day in the park, which flags they'd waved and which promises they'd made. Whatever emotion the Voices latched onto, whatever gateway into the mind they chose, it was always tailored to their victim's greatest weakness. Sadness, fear, anger, grief, shame, envy — those were the most common avenues. What emotion had they taken advantage of in Kaed, and why had it worked so splendidly?

I've made so many new friends...

When he finally realized it was loneliness the Voices had chosen, he was baffled it had taken him so long to figure it out.

#

If not for his parentage, the Helms would never have accepted Kaed as an initiate. He was forgetful and moody and among other things, struggled with several phobias throughout his childhood. He was the paradigm of what the Helms sought to eliminate: mental weakness. And he was the first to admit that. It was why he'd rejected his father's name. Donning that name, so indivisible from the ideas of strength and power, felt ridiculous. Orcadis's attempts to mold him were about as successful as trying to make a sculpture out of wet tissues. Time and again Kaed fell apart in his father's hands.

"You do it deliberately," Orcadis would say after a failed exercise or test. "I have two-thousand Iron Helms to train. I can't devote every second to your moods and whims."

And, as a mercy to his father, Kaed took the role of the spoiled, attention-seeking son, wore it like an ill-fitting cloak. He knew without having to be told that Orcadis would accept that more readily than he'd accept incompetence.

Kaed got Infected on his eighteenth birthday, while Orcadis was out of town on a recruitment mission. In Orcadis's eyes, it would be his son's most spectacular failure. The final testament of his mental weakness. Not for one moment had Kaed considered admitting it. What could he say? *I had a party, got piss-drunk, and passed out with my shutters open right before a Swarm hit?* He'd probably be unable to keep from following up with some childish remark about how this could've been prevented had Orcadis only remembered his birthday. Now the Voice that had pried his mind open recited Akkutian lore in his father's sonorous baritone.

He had no choice but to leave. Nothing would be worse than slowly wasting away before his father's eyes. Making Orcadis watch as he succumbed to catatonia. He longed for his mother's embrace, but it wasn't fair to make her witness his demise, either. Punish her for being the supportive parent.

His parents wouldn't understand why he'd gone. Orcadis would rant about his son's petulance and insubordination and overall deliberate terribleness. But Kaed had no more choice in this matter than he'd had in changing his name, or lying about his memories, or playing the spoiled attention-seeker.

#

Orcadis knew the human brain so intimately that some called him a psychic. Others called him a mind-reader. In the far reaches of the empire where superstition still reigned, countryfolk gossiped about his telekinetic and hypnotizing abilities.

In truth, he gleaned no satisfaction from his reputation. Any man with enough willpower could harness his mind's potential as Orcadis had. He liked to think that mentality made him modest, but he knew himself well enough to admit self-delusion. That rejection of accolades came from his inability to understand his own son. What would society think, if they knew the legendary Greathelm Durant couldn't keep an eighteen-year-old in check? If they knew the one mind that should be closest to his was the most foreign of all?

Somewhere in the deepest and darkest crevices of Orcadis's consciousness, he'd always known Kaed would get Infected. Perhaps that was why he'd tried so hard to train the boy. Or maybe it had all been one big self-fulfilling prophecy, and Orcadis's training was the very thing that had shattered his son's mental resilience. He couldn't consider such things often – thought suppression and pain desensitization had eliminated his ability to entertain negativity. *Ability.* It had been a long time since he'd conceived of seeing the negative as an ability.

Things were different now. Kaed had left. Orcadis knew where he'd gone. What he didn't know was if he had the strength to follow.

#

Kaed had limited time to plan his trip to Akkut. He stole more money from his father than he thought he'd need, considering he had but a few weeks to live. He mapped his route and asterisked his destination for when his memory would fail. The Voice residing in his brain had already begun depleting his mental reserves. In the three days he sat huddled in the back of a caravan, clutching his satchel of provisions to his chest, he remembered only a few hours. When the merchant swung the doors open, flooding the caravan with white sunlight, and told Kaed they'd arrived, Kaed staggered out like a drunken man.

The bustling desert town of his father's childhood was all pavilions beneath colourful tents, clay huts and sand blowing through streets. Dunes glistened on the horizon, the air was dry and crisp, and the sun pulsed down on Kaed's head, dampening the sound of his Voice.

Now that he was in Akkut, Kaed wasn't sure what to do. He supposed he'd rent a room in some inn and live out his limited days in isolation. It wasn't as if that was too far removed from his regular existence. He meandered through the streets until he happened upon a street musician, her panpipes breathing out a quivering melody. His father had played the panpipes, long ago. Kaed remembered him singing, his voice like a gentle earthquake in resonance. It was the only time Orcadis would speak Akkutian, when he sang. Vangardian words weren't expressive enough, he said. They couldn't capture the emotion.

If Kaed had one last wish, it would be to hear his father sing again.

#

Orcadis tracked down the last caravan to carry merchandise from Vangarde to Akkut. He spent days combing the desert-town's streets, asking vendors and paupers alike if they'd seen a young man with auburn curls and bucked teeth. By the fifth day, his jaw had been clenched so long he could hardly open his mouth. On the sixth, he chanced upon *The Helm of Steel*. Orcadis read those words over the inn's doorway and knew, though it was a ship's wheel and not a helmet painted on its walls.

He found Kaed alone in the adjoining tavern, hunched at the bar nursing a flagon between his hands. The other tenants must have noticed the telltale signs of his Infection, for they gave him a wide berth. He didn't turn when Orcadis called his name. In three strides Orcadis was at his side, gently turning him by the shoulder. Kaed's clouded eyes spoke of something other than alcohol. Orcadis's throat closed. And he'd been so confident in the efficacy of pain desensitization training.

Slowly, Kaed focused his eyes on his father. "You're not here."

Orcadis cupped his son's face in his palms. Rough, calloused palms, a token of the heritage he'd so adamantly rejected. "I finally am."

Kaed's mouth twitched upward, though the act seemed to pain him. "Leave, Father. Continue your mission to rid the world of the epidemic. I'm only one person." Kaed sounded so practical, so objective. Like a true Iron Helm. It should have made Orcadis proud. Instead it built pressure in his chest and behind his eyes. That pressure mounted until he felt some inner dam crack. He leaned down and rested his forehead against his son's. Then, closing his eyes, he opened the gates of his mental fortress. His mind was strong, potent, a more alluring banquet for the parasite living off his son.

But the Voice still needed an emotion as its gateway. An emotion raw and vulnerable enough to lure it out of its current habitat. So Orcadis sang. He sang the same melancholy Akkutian ballad that had made tears well in his wife's eyes, when he'd sung it for her in their youths.

He heard the Voice before he felt its invisible tendrils probing into his mind. Kaed must have felt it leaving, too, because he started struggling. But the Voice had weakened him, and Orcadis held his face firmly between his hands.

"Stop!" Kaed yelled. "What are you doing? The world needs you!"

And Kaed did manage to wrench himself free, almost toppling off his barstool in the process. But it was too late; the transfer was complete. His eyes, now their usual lucid green, dilated in horror as he stared at Orcadis. "Why would you do that? Why would you let the Voices have you?"

Like Kaed had done that day at the park, Orcadis smiled as he looked upon his son. "The Voices will never have me again."

From the Other Side

Samantha Dolan

From nothing, as it's wont to do, consciousness invaded from the periphery of the dark. An Ombre of black to grey, she found she was afraid to open her eyes. Instead, she stretched her senses out from her apparently prone body like tendrils. A slow exhale, sinking her stomach all the way down to her spine, pushing her air far, far away, and then a pause. She was at the limit but there was no rush. She let the air meander its way back into her lungs, reflated herself as if she were about to float up. But there was nothing immediately identifiable about the scents around her. It wasn't alien, it wasn't clinical, but it wasn't home.

As she sorted through the smells, her ears stretched as far as she could. In her ever-awakening mind, she saw them as calla lilies on stalks. Periscopes reaching up and out, scanning. There was the hum of silence but nothing else. Nothing she could put her finger on but without warning, the hairs on her arms rippled straight. Her ears snapped back to her heard, her breathing sped up but her eyes she held stubbornly closed. She could no longer deny the strength of the light battering through her eyelids, but her fear had taken form. Though her other senses had missed it, her soul knew for sure.

She was not alone.

There was a light tinkle of a chuckle which made her freeze. "You're alright, you can open your eyes."
It was a voice she knew she didn't recognise but felt as though she did. A combination of the weight of expectation kept her in place for a moment more but she bit the bullet, sat up and swung her body around in the direction of the voice. She opened her eyes and smiled.
"Eyebrows" she whispered.

It was a strange transition for her. It was a face she knew well. A face she'd kissed and wiped and stroked and wanted to smack for decades. But it was slightly different, the cheeks a little thinner, the nose a touch smaller. Like a slightly smudged copy...except for those eyebrows, which had always been entirely her own. The woman who sat opposite her was grown. An impossible age, considering her own, maybe in her mid-twenties but what did time mean here? She was grown and looked healthy and there was a sparkle in her eyes that mixed amusement and excitement with understanding.

This was the moment she'd been waiting for her whole life, the chance to talk to the young lady sitting opposite her. She'd rehearsed and planned and knew exactly how she wanted this moment to go so...why was she frozen?

Aeons passed. The woman never moved, the light never faded, apparently in no rush either. Maybe this was a moment they'd both been waiting for. That made her happier and she finally let her shoulders droop. Just as the words were forming, the woman rapped decisively on her knees and shot onto her feet, hand extended.

"Right! Come with me."

*

And then we were elsewhere. Sitting side by on the edge of a loch, two pairs of feet kicking lazy concentric circles out into the middle of the water. The sky was crystal clear, sparkling blue with picture perfect clouds. Perfect. Too perfect. But it would do. The companionable silence filled a void I'd never really felt the sides of before, but I was starting to be aware that as one void was being filled, another yawned behind me, waiting for me. But it could wait for now. I needed just this. We'd never been outside together before.

In the end, it was the woman who spoke first.

"I like your hair."

My hand bolted in reflex to smooth it down. "A mind of its own, but I wanted you to see it. Same colour as yours...if you ignore the grey!"

The woman winked at her. Then paused, the question being written and re-written all over her face. Finally, "What's she like?"

I smiled. "Oh, she's fierce. She's funny and kind and loyal. Smart as a whip. A complete pain in the backside but when she smiles, you'd forgive her anything."

The woman smiled her echo of a smile. "That's amazing. And the others?"

At this, I dropped her head a little. Old wounds tugged and pulled, threatening to burst open. "Sensitive. Also, loyal. Pack animals really. We all are. He's more sensitive than the other two. You girls were born with iron cores, but he's more like me. A mushy marshmallow."

The woman bumped our shoulders. "If you expect me to believe we didn't get that from you, I don't."

"Well...If I do, it's rusted."

"No, it isn't." the woman stated.

"They're a unit. And you're included. Always have been."

"Wow...that's really nice to know."

I leaned back my face, searching for the light like a sunflower. "Oh! Tell me everything. I need to know everything!"

The woman laughed her magical giggle and copied the position. "How would I even start!"

"Please..." I breathed "tell me everything. Were you lonely, were you scared? Did you hate me?" The woman stared at me as the tears flowed from my eyes to the waters, as if I alone were the source of the loch. "I'm sorry. I'm so sorry. Please. Tell me you forgive me. Please."

The woman was before me now, staring into my eyes. The brown iris with a tiny blue rim inherited from her Great Grandmother. Gently, the woman kissed my eyes to stem the flow.

"I'm not going to tell you anything if you're going to use it as a club to beat yourself. Breathe, just breathe."

The ragged breathing settled, the water calmed again, and the woman started to talk. Mindless prattle, anecdotes, yarns and tales. The woman talked of everything and nothing and every word ripped me apart and put me back together all at the same time. It was everything I'd wanted and everything she'd missed and just as the overwhelming volume of feeling threatened to crush me, the woman   stopped, sat beside me, head resting on my shoulder.

"Did you miss me?" I asked.

The woman paused for an age. "Would it hurt you if I said no?"

I smiled, "No, and yes. But largely no..."

"...but a little yes..." the woman laughed. "I don't know if we define 'miss' the same way. Missing you would imply I didn't have you. And to me, I always did."

"But...well." I stopped.

Silence descended again, and again, it was the woman who broke it. This time, it was unintentional. We sat in the water, and she began to sing. Half-forgotten lyrics about clouds, rooms full of toys, ladies dressed in white singing lullabies. While the woman carried the melody, I filled in the blanks. Remembered the quiet moment we were last together, the woman so much smaller then, smaller than she should have been to face the world. I sang again then, stroking the woman's hair as I had all those years ago. I cuddled the woman closer and we matched our breathing and for a moment, the notes floating away to the far shores, we felt at peace.

Then it was over, and we held each other again.

"I always had you, Mama." She whispered.

"If I could have..."

"You need to stop." The woman chastised gently. "You must be so exhausted. Why are you carrying this guilt?"

"Because...it's not guilt."

"No, it is. You blame yourself."

"Well, what else am I supposed to do?"

The woman slipped her fingers into my hand and squeezed. "You could put it down."

Simple. 5 words. I sighed and pulled my daughter tighter to my chest. "Yes, I could."

"But you won't." The woman giggled. "You're a lot of work Mama."

"I promised I would look after you...."

"...and you did. You do. But I need you to be there for her, and the Bigs. I need you to be ok for as long as you can for them."

From the far side of the loch, the brightness of the light could no longer be ignored. As it encroached on us from the front, we felt the yawning void arching towards us from behind. I pulled this grown, beautiful, happy woman up by the shoulders, investigated her face and ran her thumbs over her eyebrows.

"So bushy" I laughed "You can blame your dad for that."

"I'll be sure to make him apologise when I see him. But they aren't bad...are they?"

"Nothing about you is bad, my perfect little darling" I said firmly. "I'm so proud of you. So, so proud. Be happy, my angel and one day, I'll come back to stay."

She finally let a tear fall. "Not too soon please, Mama. But I'll be here."

We didn't say those three words. Instead, as the light and dark raced to embrace, we rested our heads together, lightly rubbing noses, breathing in, letting our senses cement the memory.

*

She woke. She wiggled her toes, put her hand up her nose, feeling the faint echo of an Eskimo kiss. Her head scarf had slipped off and her grey streaked hair was running kinky and free. At the end of the bed sat an ironing board groaning under the weight of unprocessed clean washing. The other side of the bed was empty, but the shower was thundering down the hall, he'd be back soon. She wondered if she'd tell him about it, but thought she'd wait and see what kind of morning he was having.

She leaned over and grabbed the video monitor, but there was no need because all the doors were open and she could hear every word. Deep discussions about who would win between Batman and Rainbow Dash. Musing on what makes a bad guy, joy at the baby giving kisses, rage at the baby kisses not being shared. Threats of being told on, tears followed by laughter followed by shouts and then back to Batman in a Batwing. She smiled, wondering when the feeling of crushing loss would replace this feeling of warmth and calm. It always did eventually but today it lingered, and she let it. She opened herself to the dynamic of her life and just allowed it to be ok for a moment.

"Mummy!"

"Mummy!"

"Mama!" They bellowed and laughed.

"Mummy! The baby needs a nappy change!!"

"She pumped!"

The three of them cackled, because what's funnier than a dirty nappy?

Heavy footsteps and a pause.

"What you sayin'?" he barks in a funny voice "Awwww, poop time is between 9 and 5 Monday to Friday. We've been over this baby!" He's gentle as he chastises, and she hears the baby giving him kisses.

"Where's Mummy? I think it's Mummy's turn for a poop." He said, already half way down the stairs.

She lies back, looks up and the ceiling listening to three, feeling all four.

I'm right here.

Stitches

Sim Bajwa

Sanya knew that people in town called it a magic shop. She supposed she should be glad that there was never any malice in their voices when they referred to her as the "witch on Mill Lane". It made a change from what her grandmother had experienced. No one was destroying Sanya's garden in the night. Nor were they scrawling "GET OUT WITCH" on her front door. Then again, the residents of Laines had never seen just what Sanya could do. And she was going to keep it that way.

She did try to discourage the townspeople from calling her business a "magic shop". She sold fabric and haberdashery, for God's sake. She had rebranded three times. But still, customers would caress the little drawers of buttons, asking if the buttons and beads were spells and curses. And if they weren't, could she possibly put a spell on a couple of needles for them? Not for any particular reason, of course. Just in case. Those ones, she reported to the police.

She really only had herself to blame. She had never *meant* to monetise her power. She truly hadn't. Magic is sacred, magic is to be used sparingly, magic is never, *ever* to be sold. Those were the rules she had grown up with, those were the words her mother had her recite every day during her training.

But it happened the first time over a year ago. Her shop assistant, John, had broken up with his girlfriend, and he just *would not stop crying*. He had scared away almost half of her customers, and Saturday was their busiest day. The knitting group that met in the shop sat in silence as John sobbed into his hands.

"Look, love," Emmaline, the oldest of the group, said. "Girls will come and go. You're young! You try to focus on yourself – "

Emmaline's voice was drowned out by John's rising wail. A man looking through the sale table jumped and dropped the roll of silk in his hands. It landed on his dog, who startled, and darted under the knitting group's table. After a flurry of screaming, spilled tea, crushed cake, and abandoned knitting, Sanya decided *enough*.

Magic is sacred. Sure. But so were her sales targets.

That evening, she stayed in the shop late, and cut out two heart shapes from a roll of crushed velvet. She pieced them together, stuffed them with wool, and sewed the edges tight with a metallic, gold thread. With the same thread, she embroidered *John* into the velvet.

And then a part of her stepped to the side, away from herself. It was always a strange experience. She was weightless, and yet anchored by her body. She couldn't move, but she could feel the cat in the alley behind the shop, she could feel Adam watching *Take Me Out* while he waited for her to get home, and most importantly, she could feel John across town, asleep on his sofa. Tears dried on his cheeks, light from the TV flashing across his face. Sanya could also feel the throb in John's chest, the sharp, twisting, disbelieving pain.

She worked quickly with her needle, stitching a neat row across the makeshift heart in her hands. And as she did, the pain in John's chest soothed, lessening until it disappeared.

She stowed the velvet heart away in her desk drawer.

The next day, John was...fine. No tears, no wailing, no heartbreak.

"What did you do to John?" Emmaline whispered, her brow creased.

"Nothing!" Sanya replied, trying to convey just the right amount of confusion and affront.

"That boy was a limp, soggy mess less than a week ago, Sanya. Now it's like nothing ever happened."

Sanya tried to stare her out. Her eye twitched. Emmaline raised an eyebrow and pursed her lips. Sanya broke.

"Okay, fine. Fine. I'll show you, but don't tell anyone."

Emmaline nodded, graciously. "I would never betray your confidence, love."

Sanya made the mistake of believing her.

When Arlene came in and lingered over rows of ribbons, Sanya didn't think anything of it. The shop was quiet, and golden afternoon light streamed in, setting the silks hanging on the wall ablaze. After ten minutes of Arlene shooting furtive glances in Sanya's direction and Sanya pretending she didn't notice, Sanya closed her laptop and sighed.

"Can I help?"

Arlene worried her lip, seemed to hesitate.

"Well, I was wondering... Sanya, you know how..."

"Sometime today would be good, Arlene."

"Emmaline said you healed John. She said you healed him, and now he's fine. Can you...could you please..."

Sanya could see where this was going. And her first instinct was *no*. Absolutely not. What would her mother say? What would her grandmother say?

But...Sanya's mother and grandmother were never small business owners.

She met Arlene's eyes and took a deep breath. She could feel the shattered hurt in Arlene's heart. The edges of the wound weren't healed over yet. In time, if left alone they would. It would be harder for Arlene to open her heart again if she allowed Sanya to manipulate it.

That was what Sanya should have said. She should have explained that an artificial healing was only a quick fix. That she shouldn't have healed John the way she did. That pain should be felt, should be learnt from, should make you wiser, stronger, more compassionate.

But when she opened her mouth, what she said was, "So, will you be paying by cash or card?"

Now, a year later, Sanya had to add another chest of drawers to her office. Every drawer was full of stitched velvet hearts. She'd had John organise them by name and then by the amount of stitches they'd received. Some people only wanted the deepest of wounds to be stitched, unable to bear the grief. Some people kept coming back.

"Arlene, there isn't any space left," Sanya said, gently.

She held Arlene's velvet heart in her hand between them, and then turned it over. Almost every inch of it was covered in gold thread, with tiny flashes of deep purple peeking through.

"Can't you make me another one?" Arlene asked. Her tone was too casual, her expression unconcerned. "My cat was run over. I have a busy month at work ahead of me. I don't need the distraction."

"Oh..uh, well." Sanya stammered. "I'll get back to you, alright?"

Arlene nodded, her attention already on her phone, as she left the shop.

Magic should be used sparingly, there is always consequence. Sanya's mother's voice flitted through her mind.

She ran her fingers over the scars she had created on Arlene's heart, and thought about the hundreds in the room behind her, and she felt a flicker of something.

It wasn't quite sadness, wasn't quite regret, but it was close. The emotions were dulled, whispered shadows of what they should have been. She knelt and reached opened the safe under the counter. Her own heart was where she had left it, tucked away to the side. She pulled it out, frowning over how frayed it was. Parts of the red velvet were worn away, and some of the stitches were close to snapping. She had stopped healing her own heartbreak years ago. The first stitch still held strong though, right through the centre of her heart. That one belonged to her mother.

Who would she have been, Sanya wondered, if she had allowed herself to feel the grief? She hadn't even cried at the funeral. It suddenly felt imperative to find out, and urgency gripped her as she pulled open her sewing case and pulled out her seam ripper. Her hand trembled as she hooked the tiny blade under the first stitch. She pulled, careful not to tear the velvet.

She had to stop after the first five stitches. Her chest hurt, and tears slipped silently from her eyes. She closed the shop early and sat behind on the floor behind the counter, bracing herself against the solid wood. It took all night.

Her eyes were puffy from crying. She couldn't move, couldn't speak, couldn't think about her mother without weeping. But with the tears came other things.

She had forgotten the sound of mum's bangles. She had owned the shop before Sanya, and she would carry incense around in the morning. The shop would smell like sandalwood. She'd loved coconut but hated coconut *on* things.

Somewhere in between the stitches, Sanya had lost more than she'd realised. She dragged herself up and opened the first drawer of stitched hearts. She had taken those things from people too. She pulled out the first one.

Jacob Allreed. Only three stitches, but one was particularly thick. His business had failed.

She sighed, gripping the seam ripper. She was going to have to give *so many* refunds.

At least Sanya still had Emmaline's knitting group. The town hated her, but the knitting group still came by – she didn't charge them to use the space for their meetings.

It had taken her three days to rip our every stitch in every heart. The first day, the town's only bank stayed shut. Mr. Arazini, the manager, hadn't made it into work. People had been worried – he was old, had a bad heart, what if something had happened? Only Sanya knew he was sitting at his kitchen table, half a bottle of cheap vodka at his elbow, thinking about the cyclist he had hit with his car three months ago.

The second day, fights had broken out in the market. Emotions were running high, and there had been whispers about people's hearts. Some believed Sanya's magic had worn off, some were convinced she was a fraud. She'd taken their money, and the effect wasn't permanent! Would she need a receipt to process a refund? Did anyone know if she *would* refund after twenty eight days?

At the end of the third day, Sanya let the seam ripper drop on her desk, her fingers aching as she stretched them. For three days, she'd barely eaten, slept in short bursts, and questioned what she was doing a thousand times.

Who did she think she was, turning down perfectly good cash? People consented to her form of 'treatment', who was she to tell the customer no?

Between the indignant justifications, she heard her mother's voice.

Magic is sacred, magic is to be used sparingly, magic is never, ever to be sold.

"Staring into space again," Emmaline muttered a week later, as she hung her coat beside the door. "Can't even be bothered to say hello."

Sanya focused on the other woman, slightly shocked to see anyone back in her shop. It had been a week of just her and John – mostly with her trying to avoid John because whenever he gazed at her with those big wet eyes, she wasn't too sure if she had done the right thing after all.

Could she at least have asked? *She* knew that a heart needed to heal on its own, but shouldn't she have left that up to her customers?

The door opened again and Emmaline moved out of the way as Judith stepped in, her knitting bag slung over her shoulder. She looked at Emmaline, then at Sanya, and then at their regular knitting table. Her mouth pulled down in a scowl, the wrinkles in her cheeks deepening.

"Where are the cakes then?" She threw an accusing look Sanya's way. "What, you're not getting us cakes anymore?"

Before Sanya could answer, the door opened again. Well, she might as well wait for them all to get here before she told them Martin Rowley wouldn't let her in his shop. He would probably come around eventually, but not until he could look at her without thinking about how he'd cried when he'd asked her to make him forget his first boyfriend. She could just send Emmaline round there. They'd serve her fine, no problem.

Sanya wasn't annoyed. Not at all.

It wasn't another of the knitting group though. It was Arlene, her eyes wild, her cheeks mottled pink.

"I told you I was busy!" Judith hustled out of the way as Arlene stalked to the till. "I told you this month was busy. I have three deadlines, four presentations, three new hires...why would you do this?"

Sanya breathed deep, placing her hands flat on the counter top. "If you follow the contact link on my website, you'll find all the information on how to claim a ref-"

"I don't want a fucking *refund*," Arlene hissed, pushing her face close to Sanya's. "I want my *life* back! I don't have time for this! I can't -" Her face crumpled in a sob and her next words came out as a garbled wail. "I was passed over for a promotion last year! I work sixty hours a week. And they. Don't. *CARE!*"

Sanya dared to reach forward and placed her fingers gently on Arlene's arm. "I know it's hard, but you'll be better for it...I know I –"

Arlene shoved away from the till, breathing too fast, a wheeze building in her chest. She held a hand up as she backed off, a fresh round of tears in her eyes. She pointed at Sanya, her finger shaking.

"*Fuck* you. Fuck you, fuck your shop, fuck all of this!"

She left, letting the door slam behind her. Sanya winced. The hinge was already damaged, and she couldn't afford to fix a broken door.

Emmaline and Judith stared at her.

"What?"

They both blinked. In unison.

"*What?*"

The door opened yet again, and three more knitting ladies walked through. Judith cleared her throat. "I'll go get some cakes, shall I? Oh no, don't even think about paying me, Sanya dear. You hold onto your pennies." As she reached for the doorknob, she added, "You'll be needing them the way things are going."

It took a month for Laines to return to almost normal. It took a further week for a customer to come in to buy fabric, instead of glaring at her through the front window. It took *another* week before she didn't feel like everyone stared at her when she went into town. People seemed to move on, as much as they were able. The were plans to build a monstrosity of a Tesco Extra on one of the most historic street despite energetic protests against it– that completely overshadowed Sanya.

Finally, three months after she'd pulled that first stitch, something shifted with John.

Sanya stood on a ladder, draping muslin for the window display when she looked down to find John staring up at her, with a grim set to his jaw.

"You know, if you're going to push me off, you might want to consider the fact that there is a witness." Sanya nodded at something out the window.

John followed her gaze to find Jethro, Mrs. Anderson's poodle tied to a bike rack outside the shop.

"I know he can't speak, but he's very intelligent. I'm sure he'd lead the police right to your doorstep."

"Shut up," John muttered, holding the ladder steady as she climbed down.

He folded the ladder and leaned it against the wall, before shoving his hands in his pockets.

"This isn't easy – "

"I'm so sorry – "

They both stopped talking and stared at each other.

"The thing is – "

"I'm really sorry, John – "

John held his hands out. "Me first!"

Sanya nodded, mentally bracing herself. If he quit...fine. He could leave if he wanted. She didn't need him. She didn't need anyone. Maybe she could bribe Adam into helping around the shop. He'd promised *in sickness and in health.* This was a broad interpretation of sickness. It's not like she had as many customers anymore. It would be *fine*.

"I don't like that you did that...thing to me without asking. And I don't like that you didn't tell me that you did, or that you didn't ask me when you undid it." He held up a hand when Sanya started to speak. "I get why you did it. And a part of me wants to say thank you." He wagged his finger when she started to smile. "A very *small* part of me wants to say thank you. Don't push it."

Sanya nodded and waited.

"I guess you've restored the...natural order of things. And for what it's worth, I think you did the right thing by unstitching."

Sanya nodded again, too afraid to say anything in case she ruined the moment.

"And you need to change the formatting on your website. The information on how to get a refund is in the smallest font imaginable."

The Lizard and the Dove

Stephanie Bowman

There once was an old man who lived deep in the showers of a green forest. He had a tidy dirt path that led over the south hill where a lake basked in the sun. At least, that's how he remembered it; he hadn't been to see the lake for many long years. In fact, he sat in his little wood cabin just as he had since then. His chair was knobby, poking a bit into his back, but he'd grown rather used to it, and he could only just remember when he'd removed the door from its hinges so he could always look out into the trees.

He thought of the lake often, but his old friend, a tiny red lizard, would always coax him to forget it. He'd met the lizard when the hinges had had a door and his knobby chair had rested in the darkest corner. He might have been happy then, but all he could remember was his daughter bringing her own children round far too often for his liking. The door was always left wide open, and the tiny red lizard had slipped in, slinked up the leg of the chair, and stopped to rest by the man's rough hand.

'Why do you let them come and go as they please?' The lizard asked.

'Because they are children,' the man replied.

'But their mother,' the lizard insisted. 'Why does she encourage them to run about and cause such a ruckus? Does she not know how tired you are?'

This was quite a surprise to the man, so he took a moment and thought. He was sure that tiny red lizard was right.

'I don't think I would have figured out such a thing on my own. I wonder if you would stay with me the rest of the day to show me what else I might have been missing.'

'Well, of course,' the lizard exclaimed. Then it wriggled up onto his shoulder so it could better whisper into his ear.

There were very many things the tiny red lizard opened the man's eyes to that day. Toys tossed across the floor, the water left running in the bathroom, and jam smeared inside all the kitchen drawers. It was amazing that the man had not noticed such annoyances before! The lizard had been such a help to him, that he invited it back the next day to continue helping sort out the utter chaos that threatened to overcome the man's home.

They found even more troubling messes, and soon the tiny red lizard wasn't returning to its own home in the evenings. It would stay up for hours with him, discussing at great length all the restrictions that must be made to all who entered through the door. At first they were only asked to remove their shoes before coming in. In a few weeks, they also had to leave their shoes on the porch, then they had to leave all their goodies and toys out as well, no nearer to the porch than the little dirt path. The man took to locking the door at the red lizard's bidding, keeping everyone out until his rules were met. He was far too proud of the improvements he and the lizard had made together to notice that his grandchildren were all silent and mopey. His daughter did not come so often and even the oldest children never smiled as they squirmed in their seats.

The last day his daughter came, he and the lizard had come to a necessary conclusion: his home was not meant for little fingers that picked up precious knick-knacks and smashed them soundly on the floor. He announced at the door that they weren't welcome inside anymore. It had felt so obvious to make the rule, yet the hurt in his daughter's eyes made him question it for a moment. But he remembered what his little red friend had reasoned and held his ground when his daughter made argument. He held firmer still when she became angry. He held tight while the little lizard whispered phrases in his ear, until his daughter vowed she would never come back while her children were banished. The two of them watched her storm away, the lizard consoling him as she went. She would see reason soon and be back to apologize. He became so sure she would come around to the truth that he removed the door from its hinges and left it leaning against the porch. He wouldn't have to worry about locking anyone out anymore.

He began to listen for her steps coming up the dirt path. Several weeks passed and he heard nothing but the wind whistling down the south hill. He found himself checking the doorway several times a day, looking out into the trees, but seeing nothing. He hardly left the cabin for fear of missing something or someone. Then he dragged his knobby chair to sit just inside the doorway, and from that moment, he never left the cabin and never moved from the spot.

Sometimes he would argue with the tiny red friend that had become so familiar in his home, so familiar on his shoulder. But it always knew so much more of the world and how things should be. The man was always set straight in the end: he was finally happy; he could do whatever he liked. More and more, he liked to do nothing but sit and look out at the trees and his little dirt path. He had his own peace and quiet right there, and happiness couldn't be more than that. How he loved to talk about everything with the tiny red lizard, unless it began to suggest the man needed some changes, too. Sometimes it could be miserable, but this was his dearest friend, and surely friends were expected to pick at one another.

Yet it seemed that the tiny red lizard couldn't stop. There was too much to put in order, and it always had to have the final say. Rather than risk his friend becoming angry, the man let himself be convinced to keep up with their improvements.

That is until one day, while the man sat in his knobby chair looking out at the trees, a beautiful white dove landed in the branches. It sang the loveliest song he had ever heard though the melody was soft because the trees were so far. He longed to invite the bird in, but it flew off after only a moment. The lizard moaned how grateful they should be that such a fanciful creature had left them in peace. Secretly, the man wished it was his tiny red friend that would be quiet.

A few days later, the man heard another sweet song and, searching the air outside, he saw the dove again. This time it looped in and out of the trees—the tiny red lizard groaning and covering its ears all the while—then perched on the porch railing for a moment before flitting off and away. Soon the man began to listen more for birdsong than the whisperings of his little red friend. Though sometimes he forgot the dove and wondered if he had missed it because he was so intent on the conversation of the lizard, he was hearing its song more than ever.

Soon it was echoing on his porch daily, inviting him out into the forest. He longed desperately to go meet it, but the tiny red lizard was his voice of reason. What friend would a silly bird be when a wise lizard was already his companion? Nothing needed to change, it would say. But the man did not quite believe the myths the tiny red lizard spouted anymore. He only wished he knew how to find out what was true.

The next morning, the man rose long before his sleeping lizard friend. He was surprised to find the dove just outside his doorway, looking in at him with steady eyes.

'Do you like my song?' The bird ruffled its feathers as he admired it.

'Yes,' he cried. 'Your song is the sweetest of any I have heard my whole life.'

The bird replied, 'You can learn to sing it again.' Then it waited.

The man was confused. 'I've never learned your song,' he answered, 'but I will do whatever I have to, so I can.'

But the tiny red lizard had come out from bed just then. The man saw its eyes go wide at what he had said. And even wider at the sight of the dove near enough to touch. The lizard rushed to him, hollering at the dove to leave. But it didn't move. It kept gazing at the man, waiting.

The man looked between the two, wishing he didn't have to choose. The tiny red lizard was so familiar and had lived with him longer than anyone, but the white dove's song reminded him of something. Something he thought he had already found? Or maybe it was something he had had long ago.

'Do you know my daughter,' he asked the dove. The tiny red lizard gasped, but his attention couldn't be stolen

'She asks about you every day.'

The lizard clung to the man's wrinkled fingers and began to speak of all the wonderful things they had accomplished through their years together. It pleaded for the man to listen, to remember what peace and happiness they had discovered inside the little wood cabin. And instead of lifting it onto his shoulder, as he had so many times, the man shook its tiny hands off.

'You've been my only friend for too long,' the man said. 'It's time that you left.'

With a final glare, the tiny red lizard scurried from the cabin, moaning and cursing at the man until it was lost in the wild grass. The man turned back to the beautiful white dove.

It fluttered its wings. 'Shall we meet them at the lake?'

The man imagined what his daughter must look like now, and how big his grandchildren must be. He took in a deep breath, seeing his empty little cabin and its dusty corners, then stepped out onto the porch. The beautiful white dove took flight, leading the way.

Magical Man-eater Makeover

Laura Gregory

Internet Search History:

12/02/2016:   How to bring the spark back into your marriage

Tart Lingerie– sexy Valentines sale on now

50 things that will drive him crazy!

01/06/2016:   Easy dinner recipes in under 30 minutes

Community adult programs – couples counselling, reading group…

Wine on sale

22/09/2016:   Wine on sale

Chocolate on sale

How to tell if your husband is cheating on you?

18/10/2016:   Jennifer Agram – negative results

Jen Agate – negative results

Jenna Argyll – intern at FSA Bank – Recent graduate, Jenna Argyll joined….

20/12/2016:   Books on sale

Present ideas for the man who's hard to buy for!

Jenna Argyll – intern at FSA Bank – Recent graduate, Jenna Argyll joined…

Cyanide

Arsenic

New turkey stuffing recipes you have to try!

09/01/2017:   Divorce Lawyers

19/04/2017:   Wine on sale

Chocolate on sale

Ice cream on sale

01/07/2017: How to love again after a divorce?

How to find men when you're over 40?

How to find love when your bastard husband cheats on you

19/07/017: Makeover advice

Karen stared at the laptop screen, wine glass in hand, watching pert young twenty-something women cover their already flawless skin in foundation and powder. There was something they did now called "contouring". It involved "bronzer" and "highlights". Some of them painted their skin with blue and green and orange smears, blending it all in until a supermodel stared back at the screen where an attractive girl-next-door had just been. Ads popped up in the corners for false eyelashes and real hair extensions. No wonder she'd struck out online dating and at that singles event Emma had dragged her to. At least she hadn't gone out in her dusty old blue mascara, then she really would have been laughed at!

Of course Richard didn't have to worry about any of this, did he? No contouring for men. They just aged, their bellies growing fatter along with their wallets, until some spunky little intern, *her* face no doubt contoured to supermodel lengths, jumped into their lap. It was all so easy for men.

Scrolling through beauty videos on Clicktube, she hovered the mouse over one where the woman looked a little older. Still beautiful, in that ageless movie star kind of way, but not caked in make-up. Something more natural. Taking a swig of wine, she pushed play.

Clicktube: Beauty Guru Lunaloup's 3 Easy Steps to a Magical Makeover!

Step One – Beauty Basics

[Transcript Starting:]

Hello my lovelies! Thank you for joining me, Luna Loup, your beauty guru, as I go over some little tips and tricks to rejuvenate your looks, regenerate your self-image, and give yourself a fabulous makeover! This is part one of my three easy steps and by the end you're going to be fierce, fabulous, and irresistible to men! I'm calling it my Maneater Makeover and I hope you join me on this journey. Remember to subscribe to follow my videos! Become a Luna member and save money as part of the Luna pack!

We're going to start with some simple tricks to cover wrinkles and blemishes, learn how to do a winged eyeliner to make your eyes pop, and how to bring out the best of your features. I've listed my favourite products and remember I'm launching my own brand, so be sure to grab them all and follow along with me!

[Pause]

Karen eyed the screen suspiciously. The woman's skin had an effortless glow. Her hair was tousled in a sexy, careless way that almost convinced Karen she hadn't spent hours styling it. Glancing down at her list of makeup recommendations there wasn't a contour sponge in sight. Maybe, maybe this could work. Staggering up to grab the wine bottle from the fridge, Karen made a detour to collect her make-up bag and a mirror.

[Play]

And that's it, my lovelies! Remember to practice-practice-practice! And then I want you to join the pack for special access to Step 2: Owning the bold look. Remember to subscribe for great savings! Much love!!!

[End Transcript]

Karen rubbed at the corner of her eye where she'd smudged the winged eyeliner so many times the skin was red. But still, her skin was smoother, she did feel younger. It could be the wine lying to her, but she stumbled up to bed with a smile on her face. Just you wait and see, Richard.

04/08/2017:

Karen had been practicing. Each time she carefully did up her face, she felt more confident. She met people's eyes in line at the shops. She dared to speak up in the big company meeting when she usually hung quietly at the back. Her make-up became a ritual, applied at sunrise in the morning, calming, peaceful. At sunset, she'd wipe it off in long, smooth strokes. And it seemed, to her at least, that her wrinkles really were fading. The bags under her eyes growing less pronounced. Which must have been wishful thinking, and yet each day when she applied it anew, it did feel like a little spell of confidence.

Her make-up bag swelled at the seams with all her newly purchased goods. Part of it came from Richard's alimony money. Not that she needed it, she had her own career, thank you very much. But damned it if she was going to let that little hussy live high on his earnings when she'd scraped and saved for years to get him where he was. A wee bit of payback was exactly what the jerk deserved. And today her collection was growing, because LunaLoup's own line of make-up had just arrived in her mailbox. She sorted out the items, seeing palettes of beautiful grey tone eye shadows, lipstick as red as blood, and suddenly she felt uncertain. A natural hue is what she had been working on, but this was maybe too much.

A handwritten card was in with the purchase. It had a password.

Pouring her wine, Karen pulled up Clicktube.

Clicktube: Beauty Guru Lunaloup's 3 Easy Steps to a Magical Makeover!
Step Two – Owning the Bold Look
Password to the Pack: ********

[Transcript Starting:]

Hello my lovelies! Thank you for joining me, Luna Loup, your beauty guru. I would like to welcome all the new members to the pack. I hope you have all been practicing and are ready to take on the sexy new look. We're going to indulge in the smoky eye, have fun with a bold red lip, and bring all the men around us to their knees. Let's get started on making you all irresistible!

[Pause]

Opening the eyeshadow palette, Karen bit her lip. This would not be the broad, bold strokes of her 80s youth. She touched the three different eyeshadow brushes that had come in the package, unsure of their intended use. But then up on the screen, there was Luna, her demeanour calm, her energy upbeat, reassuringly confident that she would lead the way, if only Karen would follow. Adjusting the mirror, Karen picked up a brush.

[Play]

And now you are all fierce goddesses, ready to approach any one you desire. As always, my lovelies, I want you to practice-practice-practice! And for those very special members of my Luna pack, remember to subscribe for access to Step 3: Beauty & Beast. Much love!

[End Transcript]

Karen glanced in her mirror – and gasped. Applying the make-up, she'd been so focused on each step, she hadn't taken in the full image. But now she did. Her eyes were sultry, heavy-lidded, as if she was just dreaming about someone. Her lips were full, with a little pout, an expression she hadn't made since her wedding night. She fumbled with her phone, checking the time. It was late, but not too late for Emma not to be up. Likely drinking her own wine, lamenting her own divorce. And wasn't she always pestering Karen to go for a night out? Karen was sure she'd love to go, no matter how late the hour.

08/09/2017:

Three dates a week for the last month. Karen had done well. It seemed no matter where she and Emma went, the men flocked to her, filling her phone with their numbers. It had come to the point Emma was jealous, refusing to take her out, but that was fine, she went alone. She slinked her way through the night, meeting doctors and lawyers. The men could be deep in crowds of younger women, and yet when she walked past, a swing in her hips, a strut in her step, they followed her. Jostled and pushed for her attention. It was gratifying, at first, the flirtations, the attention. It was what she imagined rich older men felt like, flocked by attractive women. It should have felt like justice, but there was a gnawing problem at the back of her mind: none of them were Richard.

If Richard could see her surrounded by them, perhaps that would do. As far as he knew, she was still the poor lonely divorcee trapped at home. No, she needed him to know she was fabulous. She needed an excuse to drop back into his life. Give him a taste of what he was missing. So she ransacked the house and found old boxes up in the attic. Sentimental things they had put there after their final move from the threadbare flat to the sumptuous house and promptly forgotten about. So she dragged it all down, awash in nostalgia and regret, bitter like she hadn't felt in weeks.

This wasn't the way she wanted to meet him. She could not face another defeat. Lost, she poured another glass of wine and sought out her mentor, her leader. Logging onto LunaLoup's beauty site, she clicked for the third and final step. Willing to pay whatever exorbitant price was demanded, she was shocked to see there was no number. Instead, there was a text field, glaringly empty.

Luna wanted the reason the subscriber wanted to be an irresistible man-eater.

Karen stared at the screen.

[Text Field:]

~~As a lover of your product, I would very much like~~

[Delete]

~~Hi Luna, I'm a forty year old divorced woman and~~

[Delete]

…REVENGE…

[End Text Field]

The parcel arrived the next day.

09/09/2017:

This one was different. There was no make-up. Not that it mattered. Now, no matter how hard Karen scrubbed her face, the smoky hue would not fade. Her lips were stained crimson. Her skin was nearly as flawless as Luna's and she had not applied a spot of concealer in weeks. She opened the box to see a set of lacquerista false nails, as long and sharp as talons. Another box held novelty contacts, they were silver and mesmerized her with their shine. As before, there was a handwritten card.

Clicktube: Beauty Guru Lunaloup's 3 Easy Steps to a Magical Makeover!
    Step Three – Beauty & Beast
    Password to the Pack: ***************

[Start Transcript:]

Hello my lovelies. I am so pleased to welcome you to the inner circle. You should know that you are the chosen few. My special pack. I promised to make you all irresistible and now is the time to fulfill that promise. I hope you have all been appreciating the changes that have come your way. There is just one final step. One last ritual and then everything you wanted will be yours. Open the parcel and you will see a set of acrylic nails….

[Pause]

Karen spilled her wine. It was hard to pick up with the claws on her fingers. The screen hurt her new eyes, so she looked away from Luna's beautiful face. But what caught her attention was a scent, coming from the boxes from the attic. Something familiar. Someone she used to know. Stalking to the box, she rummaged until she found it. Richard's shirt, heavy with his scent. Grabbing her keys off the table, she held the shirt to her nose. The hunt had begun.

The Two Brothers

C.J Skye

The girl careened down the steps to the marina, small blue backpack bouncing on her shoulders with every bold leap. She loved the quie0t of late September mornings, when the tide of tourists was on the ebb, but the last beach umbrellas still dotted the Vietri shore. *Like mechanical sunflowers*, she thought, *blooming to hold the last warmth of the year close to the ground.*

If she hurried, she'd be the first of her family to make it down to the beach, and have the rare chance to read a bit before her toddler brother could crawl and grab her hair in pudgy fingers, perhaps even take a swim and lie in the sun before he'd shovel sand all over her towel.

In the distance, a spray of seagulls courted a fishing boat with sharp, longing cries. The girl turned to look at them, and a gust of wind sent a tangle of black locks to cover her eyes. She giggled, contented. She loved the tickling of her curls, impractical as they were. Growing her hair out had marked a momentous victory, her right at twelve to style her own look.

The girl trotted on to the marina's newsstand– a crammed little shop selling everything from toys, sunscreens and rubber dinghies to magazines and paperbacks, a summer's worth of reading packed in narrow shelves waiting for her to sift through. But the shop's shutters were drawn, the newspaper stalls still covered in plastic and neatly folded against the front wall. Two inflatable swim rings – bright pink with white sunflowers and green with yellow dolphins – had been left hanging from the evening before, and bounced with the gusty wind over the entrance. The girl sighed, dismayed. She considered trying her luck with the little town's other bookshop. But that took a steep walk uphill. *And chances are this one near the beach opens earlier anyway,* she reasoned. Maybe she had enough money on herself to buy an ice-cappuccino and wait in the nearest cafe for a while? She rummaged in her bag, drew out a blue, whale shaped pouch and unzipped its smiling mouth. Spreading the coins on her palm, she counted enough for that mystery novel she'd wanted, with a grand two-euro to spare. *No sitting down then*, she calculated, *but still enough to grab a treat at the counter.* She took to the wide boardwalk on the beach, a girl with a plan. And that's when she saw the old woman.

Her bent shape had emerged from the far edge of the marina, under the shade of the Aragonese watchtower and the tall tufa arches embedded in the cliffs. She moved in short, difficult steps, layers upon layers of grey-brown rags puffing in the breeze, her shoulders hunched and her head hung low. A strange flock of birds – sparrows and small gulls, blackbirds and turtle doves and starlings and robins and goldfinches - surrounded her, some flying some hopping, chirping and cawing and squawking. The girl walked her way, fascinated. With a low, cooing sound, the old woman rattled a pouch in her gnarled hands. As she drew nearer, she gave off a wild stench of bird droppings and unwashed clothes. The girl backed a step at the smell, uneasy. And the old woman raised her head, as if feeling the touch of that young gaze.

"Seeds! Seeds for the birds!" she called, her voice dry and croaking. The girl still held on to the coins for her clandestine snack. She knew her mother wouldn't approve of her love for coffee, iced or otherwise, and she wouldn't get another chance soon.

"Seeds!" went the woman, and scattered another handful on the pavement between them. The motley flock erupted in a flurry of colored wings.

"Uhm... sure," the girl decided, and resigned her small treasure.

Up close, the woman looked ancient, her nails dark and broken, the fingers of her hands twisted and stiff, and yet her movements were swift in making the offered coin disappear inside her many-layered rags.

"Have you got something to drink or a candy I can suck on, my dear? My throat is so dry."

The girl gave a quick nod, while rebuking herself for having been afraid of a frail old wanderer. She offered the small bottle of water she'd squeezed next to her towel. Sifting through her backpack also produced a couple of the propolis candies her mother always equipped everyone with in hopes of warding off throat aches.

"You're very kind, young one."

The old woman offered her bag of seeds in return, even as the girl shook her head.

"You keep that. It's ok."

"I'm not a beggar, dear. This is yours now. A gift for a gift, and no debts left outstanding." The girl didn't want to upset her, so she accepted the little canvas pouch. The wind from the sea did nothing to alleviate the stench coming off her rags. But the birds surrounded them both with chatter and song, now. And the old woman's eyes were sharp and shiny as she cooed to that mismatched flock and demonstrated the swift, gentle movement to feed it.

"Gently, now..."

The girl threw a handful of seeds to enthusiastic pecking. From the nearest sea stack, a couple of blue larks took flight from their nests and joined the ones on the sidewalk, circling her and singing. She laughed, happy, all uneasiness forgotten.

"See? They like you."

"These seeds must be very special."

The old woman stretched her leathery wrinkles in a smile.

"They are worthy of the great gryphon, dear," she replied. The girl looked up.

"The gryphon?"

"The greatest beast to ever cross the sky," the old woman revealed. "It used to be famous around here. When I was younger, people sang ballads on the hunters trying to capture it, told hushed stories by the fireplace of the bird's great magic." The light of a distant youth warmed her sharp features.

"You mean a gryphon used to live here?"

"Oh yes, my chick. This is a land of many tales."

The girl seemed to hesitate a moment, debating to herself how good an idea that was, making friends with a ragged stranger. *Mom would flip out if she ever found out*, she knew. Then she gathered the courage to ask anyway.

"Tell me about it."

The old woman unwrapped a candy to suck, and nodded.

* * * * *

There was a King once. His name is not important, kingdoms come and go on these shores, and leave little more than crumbs of their vanity in their wake. What matters is that this King was much loved by his people, and that one day he became very ill.

The best doctors in the land were summoned. They flocked at his bedside, but despite all the dignity in their Latin formulations, nothing they attempted seemed enough to help. The King soon became too weak to stand, and even his sight began to darken.

Once all hope in medicine had been lost, every mage, shaman and witch hiding in the wild was brought to court. They came and went, night after night, hidden under cloaks of twilight and stars, in through secret doors and subterranean archways, led by the Lord's most trusted knights up to the royal rooms. But they too, despite all the gravitas of their arcane chatter, seemed helpless.

No one could find a cure. Until an old, wise forest witch examined the king, and nodded in understanding.

"This illness that afflicts you isn't mundane in its nature, my Lord. There's magic at work here, so only magic shall heal you." Under the worried gazes of pages and nobles, she snatched a piece of coal from the room's hot fireplace, and scratched the smooth stone under the king's bed in an intricate pattern, with symbols so powerful the air sighed and shook in the entire castle.

"This will lend you some time." Satisfied, the old witch patted her hands clean, leaving smudges of soot on the bed's golden brocades. No one dared complain, for the King's breathing had finally eased. He gathered enough strength to speak his first words in days.

"What will it take then, my wise witch?"

"You need to fetch a feather from the great Gryphon, my King, and brush it on your eyes. This will lift the curse, and you will be healed."

The King nodded, relieved. But before he could call on his best hunters to capture the beast, the witch warned him.

"This task has to be accomplished by your own blood for this remedy to work. There is no cheating with the rules of magic."

As he was too weak to attempt the quest himself, the King had his two sons gather at his bedside.

They were so unlike each other, these two brothers. The older one, the Crown Prince, was tall, bold and strong, admired by all for his prowess with sword and bow. The younger one was a thin and sweet boy, kind of heart and manner, who seldom left the company of his books or the shelter of the castle's terraced gardens.

The King studied both with the same undisguised pride.

"My beloved sons, if I am to be healed, you'll have to embark on a journey fraught with danger." Both rushed to agree to any effort to save him. But the King shook his head, cautious.

"In the easternmost reaches of our land, up in the mountains, there lies a forest in which the great Gryphon is said to nest. I need one of its silver feathers, gained by your skill and cunning, to break the curse that is consuming me."

The two brothers had listened to the tales on this creature. The Gryphon was majestic as it was feared. Said to wield power over earth and skies, its nest woven in gold threads, the shadow of its great wings in flight could make the land it touched thrive. These and many more stories they'd heard. So they knew it also as a feral monster that would devour any mortal who'd dare venture in its forest.

"I will never leave your father's side," promised the witch "But with all my effort, I can only borrow so much time. You must make haste."

The Princes took in the bent, unrefined old creature roosting beside their father and nodded, in silence. The King had a grave look in his eyes. The whole room seemed to hold its breath, as in a thin voice he croaked his promise.

"On the one who will succeed, I will entail my entire inheritance, for he will be truly worthy of the rule of the land."

The nobles and knights gathered there were solemn and silent, witnesses to the dying King's will. Kneeling to receive their father's blessing, the two Princes vowed to honor his command, at all events, even if time had to steal their chance of saving him.

And so they left, on the fastest horses the castle had to give. Together, they rode a whole night and a whole day, until they reached the crossroads to the last town before the mountains. The eldest Prince stopped his horse then.

"We should part company now, so our chances of finding the creature will increase."

The boy eyed the impenetrable wilderness draping the cliffs, and though frightened, agreed.

"Wait till the morning to challenge this part of the journey," advised the older brother "Get some rest, buy provisions in town. You'll be alone, and are no hunter."

The boy heard the thin note of scorn in his brother's voice, and decided he couldn't be left behind.

"I'm capable of doing my part to help father."

The older Prince warned him of the dangers of the mountain then, told him not to be stubborn, but the boy would not be swayed.

"I know you mean this for my own sake. But we've both taken a vow, so we'll both do our best."

The Crown Prince watched his younger brother lead his mare deep into the forest.

"He's so eager to prove himself worthy of the throne," he scoffed. The boy had no hope of succeeding alone, of course. At this pace, he'd soon overexert his horse and be stranded. Their ride had been a rough one, and he saw no need to be so reckless. Well, things would all turn out fine, one way or the other, he reasoned.

So the older brother turned his brown stallion around and headed for the nearest town, looking for a good inn to get some rest, a decent stable, and maybe some pleasant company for a night or two.

Meanwhile, the boy rode on.

The paved road that had led him to the edge of the forest soon thinned into an ancient, overgrown track snaking through the trees. The boy followed its turns, first riding, then by foot, leading his golden mare through protruding roots and tangled branches. Horse and rider went on for days, until the roof of leaves overhead was so thick they were moving in constant shadows, and the food he'd brought along was almost all gone.

At the end of another long day in the mountains, the boy stopped to camp in a small, protected dell. As dusk set in, the shrill cries of the night hunters rose around him, and not for the first time, the boy wished his brother could be there at his side. The boy groomed his horse with care, raised a small campfire, and was arranging what little he had left to eat, when a rustle from the near darkness made him start.

"Who is it?"

A thin old man emerged from the trees, with clothes so worn and caked in mud there was an hem of moss growing on his sleeves and collar.

"I didn't mean to startle you, traveller. I saw the fire and thought that any who'd ventured this far might not shun some company." The old man was too dignified to ask for food, his eyes only flickered for a moment to the hard cheese and tangerines the boy had laid on an open napkin. With his own stomach grumbling with hunger, the young prince invited the stranger to share his fire and meal.

"It'll be pleasant to have another voice other than my own to greet the night."
And so they ate, and talked, and both banished some solitude for a while. When morning came, and the Prince was about to bide his farewell, the old man revealed a bag of seeds he'd kept tucked away, warm over his heart, safe under his many layers of rags.

"I know you came here looking for the great Gryphon, my boy," he said, and his toothless smile was so earnest the prince couldn't deny it. "I'm glad to repay your hospitality." The man handed him the bag of seeds like a small, dear treasure.

"To claim one of its feathers, ride east. Go up these slopes through the gentle beeches, and keep walking until you find a round glade where a tall, red-leaved tree stands alone, as the pupil in the open eye of the mountain. Be there at the very break of dawn. Then take these seeds, and pour them over your head, like this." He brushed the sparse white hair of his scalp with bony fingers, miming the shape of a pointy hat. "Keep very still, and wait. The Gryphon will find you. It will lean over your shoulders and feed off the seeds. Don't be afraid, and while it eats, close a hand round one of its feathers. Hold tight, so when it flies away again the feather will come loose. And since every deed deserves to be requited, the great Gryphon will let you go."
The boy thanked the old man for his advice, and rushed to follow his instructions. He'd grown more and more worried for his father's health with every passing day.

Just as he'd been told, the boy found the red tree. He waited for the break of dawn, poured the seeds over his head. As promised, the Gryphon came. Its great wings cast a shadow so huge it covered the entire clearing, but the creature landed with effortless grace on the boy's shoulder. While it fed, tingling his hair with its great beak, the boy closed his hand as tight as he dared on one of its long, beautiful feathers. And when the great Gryphon took off, the boy was left with his prize.

Spurring his mare as fast as he could, the young prince dashed down the mountain, eager to reach the palace where his ailing father waited. But as soon as he'd hit the paved road, just past the crossroads to the first town, he recognized his brother's bent shape in the distance. The older Prince had lost his horse, and his splendid clothes were ripped and dirty. His brother had spent days and nights drinking and brawling in the town's inns, and had gambled his very last coin away.

Not knowing this, and seeing his haggard face, the boy jumped off his horse and ran to hug his brother, the Gryphon's feather brandished high for him to see.

"Take heart! We haven't failed, father will be healed!"

The older Prince looked at the boy's exultant face and knew that his right to inherit land and title was lost.

"You have done very well," he said. But when the boy turned to adjust his bags so they could ride back home together, the Crown Prince picked up a stone from the side of the road and hit his brother on the back of the head, killing him.

"The kingdom is mine by right, little brother. I can't let you take everything away from me. But our father will be healed, on this you have my word."

The Prince stole the feather out of the boy's delicate hands, and carried him deep into the woods, where he buried him under an old yew tree at the edge of a small glade.

He rode back home, and triumphantly handed the feather to the King. As foretold by the witch, the curse was lifted, and his father was healed. The older son had proven to be the righteous heir to the kingdom, and all seemed well.

But in his heart, the King could never find peace, because his youngest son hadn't returned. Night after night he gazed at the dark road, hoping to see his beloved boy ride back, the lamp at his window always burning, so the light could guide him home. But his son was lost forever.

Years went by.

It was a hot day of Spring, and the sun blazed over the mountains. A young shepherd ventured into the woods, looking for some quiet, shaded little glen for his flock to spend the day in. He followed a trail for a while, until he found a nice round clearing sheltered under the branches of an old yew tree.

The grass looked green and tender, birds sang in the air, butterfly fluttered between wildflowers. So the young shepherd chose a mossy nook and settled there, contented.

His sheep started grazing, but his dog just wouldn't settle. It trotted up to the yew tree, and whined and barked to get his master's attention. Then it began digging. Curious, the young shepherd neared. He stroked the dog's matted white fur, held its strong shoulders in his hands. The dog had unearthed something. A slender white bone. The shepherd picked it up, and decided it had to be part of some old animal carcass. So he traded it with his dog for a piece of tough bread, and went back to his nook at the edge of the clearing, where he started working on it.

He carved and polished the bone, until he'd turned it into a smooth white flute. But when he blew in it, the sweet voice of a boy sang out to the sunlit woods.

> "Oh young shepherd
> Who's me to his lips,
> Hold me tight and don't let me go.
> For a silver Gryphon's feather
> My own brother became a traitor.
> And he slew me and he hid me,
> Under this grass alone to rest."

Startled, the young shepherd held the flute reverently in his hands. He didn't know whose voice that could be. But he knew that this magic he'd found in the woods had to be shared with others.

And so the shepherd began travelling through towns and villages, playing the flute and living off the charity of amazed crowds. Soon enough, word of the singing bone reached the palace, and the King asked the young shepherd to Court.

Before the rich nobles of the land, in a hall with velvet tapestries and flapping banners, the young shepherd stood.

"Show me this miracle," ordered the King. The boy had his throat dry with fright, so he handed his lord the flute with a reverent bow. And when the King blew in it, again the voice flew out.

"Dearest father

who's me to his lips,

hold me tight and don't let me go..." The King recognized at once the voice of his youngest son. With his heart breaking, he listened to the terrible tale of his boy's murder.

Heart clenched with dread, the King summoned his eldest son.

"Play this flute," he ordered. The Prince caught the tremble in his father's voice, the anger simmering there, but didn't dare refuse. And when he blew through the smooth instrument, the song filled the halls one last time.

"Trusted brother

who's me to his lips,

hold me tight and don't let me go.

For a silver Gryphon's feather,

to us all you became a traitor.

And you slew me and you hid me,

under the grass you laid me to rest."

Ashen white, the crown Prince listened to his dead brother's voice as it sung that damning accusation before the Court. The King, furious, disowned his elder son and for his crimes had him bound in a barrel sealed in tar, and thrown off the cliffs into the raging sea.

Where the barrel plunged into the waves, the water shrank away in horror, and from the foaming sea there emerged two sea stacks. One was dark and steep and ragged, for the merciless older brother, and the other one was gentler, covered in flowers and birds' nests, for the boy. They are the Two Brothers off the coast of Vietri, the cruel heir, and the sweet young prince.

* * * * *

The girl's gaze went to the sea, at the gulls and flowers coloring the two large sea stacks under the cliffs, reading the gestures of the crone's thin hands.
"Are those the ones?"
The old woman nodded.
"These rocks are still called the Two Brothers, even if most people don't remember why anymore."
The girl ran her fingers through the seeds, pensive.
"Do you think this story is true? That the Gryphon was ever real?"
The old woman nodded.
"Some things are ancient, my chick, they've always been around and still will be when even this era is long gone."
"So what happened to the King?"
"He adopted the young shepherd as his own son, as a reward for bringing him the truth on his poor boy's fate. I'm told their reign was peaceful and wise."
"It's sad, tough."
"Perhaps. But some things can be both sad and beautiful," she said, looking at the two rocks lapped by the sunlit waves "You remind me of that young prince, you know? Kind and brave fledglings, the both of you."
The girl scattered the last seeds to the birds. A screech of grinding metal announced the beach shop was opening. So she took her leave from the old woman, and quietly walked long the boardwalk, the lilt of the ballad haunting her steps.

The wind rose in gusts from the sea, tangling her dark locks, tugging at her dress. It blew through the cracks and fissures of the sea stacks, and carried the sweet voice of a boy singing. The girl turned around, and the ancient woman was still hunched in the distance, moving away in short, difficult steps. The wind got hold of her rags, and for a moment, spread them as the silver and brown feathers of a great Gryphon's wing.

Recollection

Lesley Macniven

May 12th 2018

Dear Dad,

Belated Happy Birthday.

Anna remembered your birthday was coming up and made you another lovely card.

Facebook reminded me recently too of the anniversary of your move into the care home, the sadness lifted slightly by the joke that Anna's precious bunny stayed to comfort you that first night.

I said that to stop her lip quivering and help her finally sleep.

She's grown so much, eleven now. You'd hardly recognise her. But I know you'd be as proud of her achievements as you were of mine.

We still count your birthdays too.

Xx

When A Scoundrel Calls

Megan Duff

Gina was on her second coat of nail polish, her favourite rosy nude, when the phone started ringing.

Not her work phone, her *secret cell phone*.

On a jolt of excitement she dove across her desk to grab the phone from underneath a stack of brochures. It took a few moments of playing hot potato before she had it pressed to her ear.

"Hello," she said, already breathy.

"Hey, darling," the voice said at the other end. That raspy, rumbling voice that made her feel like she was sinking into a Jacuzzi. "You got a minute?"

She shifted her shoulder to hold the phone as she pulled up all the screens she'd need on her computer. Her fingers flew carefully over the keys to avoid smudging her manicure.

"I've got as many minutes as you need." Jeez, that sounded better in her head. "But just give me a sec."

Gina twisted in her desk chair to survey the travel agency. It was a slow day, only a few appointments in the morning. The two senior agents were on lunch, which left...

"Carrie!"

Her desk mate jumped, knocking over an Eiffel Tower snow globe. The junior travel agent cringed as she addressed her trainer. "Yes?"

"Go get coffee. A mocha for me."

"But, we still have twenty—"

"It's dead. I'll cover the phones."

Carrie's brow crinkled. "But you're on a call right now."

"Exactly. Now hurry I'm wasting away."

Carrie moved like a sloth as she gathered her coat and purse. On the other end, Gina could hear heavy breathing that kicked up her pulse another notch.

"Don't you dare forget the rewards card this time!" she yelled for good measure as the door swung closed.

Fingers itching with anticipation Gina turned back to her computer. "Okay, where are we going today?"

"Hhmm," A few muffled pops and shouting. "I was thinking somewhere warm. Secluded."

"How about the white sand beaches and turquoise waters of the Maldives?"

"A hut on the beach." She could hear the smile in his smoky voice. "With you lounging in a hammock when I arrive?"

A giggle escaped her professional act. "I wish. You never tell me about these trips in advance."

"A real shame. Hazard of the job unfortunately."

Biting her lip, Gina did a flight search. She'd never asked what his job was, although she had a pretty good idea.

"Layover in Singapore?"

"Yes, at least four hours."

"Got it. Flying out of La Guardia?"

"No, make it JFK. Gotta avoid Central Parkway."

Interesting. "All right there's a flight leaving at 2:40. Can you make it?"

"Have I ever given you reason to doubt me?"

No, never. Not since that fateful day in October when she picked up a random call on the agency phone. He had been in a horrible rush, and at points she couldn't hear him over what sounded like water. He promised to thank her properly before abruptly hanging up. Ever since, the first of every month, a six-figure sum was deposited into her account from a memorial trust for someone she'd never heard of.

"Under what name?"

"What do you think? Anthony Cole or Isaac Rasmussen?"

It was always different, but he'd never given her a choice. "Anthony Cole…it's sexier."

His laugh zinged through her whole body. "Good to know. You ready for the passport number?"

She made an effort to concentrate as she typed in all the personal info. After that first call a young man came to the office to see her. He told everyone he was tech support but Gina knew better when he slipped her a jewelry box with a note. *To keep you safe, darling*. The man spent an hour uploading god knows what and left a cell phone behind on her desk. She matched her outfits to the ruby earrings but stopped Googling weird stuff. And she never mentioned her mystery client to anyone.

"Booked." She slumped back in her chair, the edge wearing off. "I'll have a driver pick you up in the Maldives."

"Actually book me a rental. Something fast."

"Will do. The address of your accommodation will be in the GPS."

"You think of everything. Are you sure that sad sack deserves you?"

The tiny diamond sparkled on her left hand. She never told him about Greg, he just knew. "I guess we'll see."

"And there's nothing I can do to steal you away?"

"Well…" Gina held her breath. "You could take me with you next time."

There was a rush of voices on the line. "I wish, darling. Maybe someday, maybe. I've gotta—"

The line disconnected. Air released slowly through her stiff lips. She brought down the phone. The call had taken less than five minutes.

Setting her shoulders she pulled together the rest of the trip. She booked him at a five star resort, a private hut just as he'd said. Looking at the pictures she paused at a shot of the large outdoor shower. She imagined him standing under that hot spray. His face was blurry but his body was clearly defined, cut. Dirt and blood colored the water at his feet and he turned to her, hand outstretched…

The bell on the door jingled as Carrie returned, huffing as she balanced a drink carrier. Gina hurried to finalize everything —a last minute bottle of whiskey added to his room, it seemed like something he'd like — and sent all the vouchers through the right channel.

Then she grabbed her mocha and left Carrie to man the office while she made her way to the break room. There she pulled a chair up in front of the dinky TV and flipped through the news channels.

Robbery. Double homicide. Hostage situation. Explosion at a junkyard.

He could be any of them. It kept her awake at night, thinking about what he was involved in. Not small stuff. It had to big.

Big enough to need an escape route across the world, and her to clear the path for him.

Maybe she'd pack an away bag and keep it at her desk.

She never knew when he might need her.

Rosemary, Rosemary

Lidia Molina Whyte

The sprigs were all wrong. They were of mismatched lengths, and not svelte enough. The needles should've been thick and soft, like the hairs of a new paint brush. Instead, they wilted away from the stems. The colour was all wrong too. They should be the green of Sierra Nevada at the dawn of spring, or La Paca's eyes drilling into you when you told a lie. Nothing like the sprigs current shade of ash.

Maybe Sofia hadn't cut them properly. Or maybe the plant had turned against her. Someone must've given her the evil eye. It wouldn't surprise Sofia if Fatima had done it. Her sister did have a knack for curses.

Sofia could picture the look Fatima would give the sprigs. Nothing made Sofia angrier than that look. She knew all the cues that preceded it too. There was the smallest of lifts in Fatima's thin eyebrow, and the faintest wrinkles around her hazel eyes. Then she would unleash the full force of her gaze upon whatever it was she was studying, carving out its faults, rendering it small and insignificant. No words to soften the blow, or give it shape; Fatima saved her words for cursing and singing, and even then, they were far and few between.

That look would be on every wall and every surface of Sofia's beloved flat. All the years of hard work it had taken her to save up the money for it would be reduced to nothing. Yes, it was small and overpriced. And there was a draft. But Sofia loved it, and she'd bought it all on her own, pouring into it every painting, print and sculpture she sold.

Sofia went to the bay window and lit a cigarette. She watched London rage by, each puff soothing away her frustration. She was being ridiculous. It had been Fatima who had suggested the visit. She wanted to bless Sofia's new home. And maybe that's why Sofia was so nervous. This was Sofia's own little slice of the world, and there was a reason it was so far away.

With the taste of smoke still thick on her tongue, Sofia went to look for her mother's sewing kit. Better safe than sorry.

***

Though Mama had taught Fatima and Sofia how to bless with rosemary and ward off the evil eye with red thread, it had been La Paca who'd told them about its other power. The power to link people's fates.

La Paca told the best stories. Tales of *gitanas* that soared the seas and wielded magic. Heroines that created their own destiny. And though she was kind to the other children, she was kindest to Fatima and Sofia. Every Saturday, they ran to her fruit stall in the best corner of the market. She always had a bag of loquats ready for them – "the ripest of the crop," she'd say with a wink – and a host of rare, beautiful books they could marvel at.

Gitanos loved to gossip about it. The girls' parents wondered, too. Maybe it was because she saw her own girls, who passed after the war, in Fatima and Sofia. Or maybe she'd sensed something in the girls' future that drove her to reach out – La Paca had a knack for these things. Whatever the reason, she doted on them lovingly, and kept two little plastic stools by her table just for them. That's where they were sitting, fingers and chins sticky with loquat juice, when she told them about the red thread of destiny.

"An invisible red thread links those who are destined to find each other, regardless of time, place and circumstance," La Paca said, peeling a loquat and keeping a sharp eye on a *paya* who was squeezing a cherimoya. "The thread can stretch and shrink, but it will never break."

"You mean we're connected?" Sofia asked, leaning so close to La Paca she almost fell off her stool.

"You are," La Paca laughed, helping her up. "From here, to here."

She traced a line from the red thread tied around Sofia's left wrist, climbing up her pinkie and floating all the way to Fatima's hand.

"And, if you have the gift, and you look through here," she pointed at a spot below her brow, "you'll be able to see the thread… Lady! They're cherimoyas, not stress balls."

La Paca shuffled over to the *paya*, leaving the girls to study their wrists. Fatima was barely ten years old and already suspicious of the world. She regarded their hands in that piercing, quiet way of hers, weighing La Paca's words with careful consideration.

Sofia closed her eyes, channelling all her scrawny eight-year-old body's energy towards the spot below her brow, just like La Paca had taught her. When she opened them, it was there; a line, bright red like the lasers Tete Manuel sold to tourists on the beach, joining her wrist to her big sister's. Its glow was so strong it almost hurt to look at. But looked Sofia had. Every night, when Fatima sang her to sleep, Sofia saw the thread. There it was, when Fatima cursed the *payos* who bullied Sofia at school, or when she lent Sofia her lucky hoops for a test.

Sofia saw the thread, time and time again, until the day Fatima married Rafael. After that, she hadn't looked for it again.

***

It had been a year of firsts for Fatima. First time she'd sung in a real venue, ticketed and everything. Frist time she'd let anyone look after her girls for more than a couple of hours while she worked overtime. First time she'd been on a plane.

The flight had been even scarier than the concert. At least the lights of the small auditorium had been dimmed, and it was all for a good cause. There had been nowhere to hide on the crammed plane, no way to blend in or disappear. It had felt as if the cabin were closing in on Fatima, and all she could do was sit there, vulnerable and exposed.

"It's not scary at all" Gracia, her eldest, had reassured her the night before. "You're literally on top of the world! And sometimes you get free food."

Fatima had looked to Alba, who was only three minutes and forty-seven seconds younger than Gracia, but every bit the little sister.

"I don't like it, Ma," Alba had muttered, tugging at the red thread tied around her wrist. "It isn't natural for something to stay in the sky like that. Plus, it smells weird. And the food is disgusting!"

Fatima had folded her mother's manila shawl for the third time, just to give her shaking hands something to do. When Gracia thought Fatima wasn't looking, she shot her sister a warning look.

"I mean," Alba had backtracked, "it's not that bad. Not really. The… water is nice."

"Seriously, Alba?" Gracia had buried her head in her hands. "The water?"

The memory made Fatima smile. At least her girls weren't like her. Barely sixteen and already they'd seen more world than Fatima ever would. She'd taken every extra shift at the hotel, and cleaned rich *payas*' houses after work too, just to make sure of it. They hadn't missed one school trip, no matter how expensive, and they'd already visited Sofia twice.

Fatima tugged at her own red thread, digging her nails into the flesh beneath. Spending time alone with Sofia was another first, the one she feared the most. Oh, they'd seen each other plenty of times since the accident. Sofia always came back for Christmas, and a whole month in the summer. But the girls or La Paca were always there to act as buffers. Without them, Fatima would have no choice but to face her sister head-on. Because Sofia was always looking for a fight, words sharpened and ready to throw at anyone foolish enough to get in her way.

Fatima shook her head and walked towards the exit, suitcase trudging behind her. This time would be different. Because even if Sofia couldn't forgive her, Fatima had finally forgiven herself.

***

Fatima was a year younger than her daughters when it was decided she would marry Rafael. He was twenty-two. They met at her cousin's wedding. She sang a tangos and everyone got up to dance. Everyone save Rafael. He'd looked at her like starving children looked at La Paca's loquats, licking his lips and flexing his fingers. After that, he was there everywhere she sang, finding excuses to talk to her, mistaking her silence for encouragement.

Papa got the call not long after. Rafael would be asking for her hand on her birthday. The family was ecstatic. Rafael was the son of gold dealers from two towns over, the kind of well-to-do *gitanos* you only dreamed your daughter would marry into. Nobody asked Fatima what she dreamed of. Rafael had the family's blessing, and that was all that mattered.

Fatima knew this day would come. She had been prepared for it her whole life. And yet, she couldn't help but feel disappointed. Deep down, she had dreamed about soaring seas and wielding magic. About creating her own destiny, just like the heroines in La Paca's stories.

Of course, it was Sofia who spoke against it. Already she wielded words like weapons, and she fought for her sister with everything she had. But, for once, Papa was immune to her bullets. This was their people's way and no amount of Sofia's impassioned speeches would change that.

The night before her birthday, Fatima wiped Sofia's tears and sang her to sleep, stroking her sister's short, spikey hair – another of her rebellions. Fatima hadn't meant to curse them; Mama and Papa were only doing what they thought was best. And yet, the lullaby she was singing turned into something darker without her realising. For the first time, she felt envious of her sister. Of how she always got her way, whether it was about not missing school to help Mama clean and cook, or going to a painting class full of *payos*. Because Mama and Papa had Fatima, who would always do what was expected of her, so Sofia wouldn't have to. She thrust all that pain, all that hate, out into the world, wishing her family could feel it too, until she finally fell asleep.

The next day, the family came together to celebrate. Sofia didn't leave her room in protest. Fatima let herself be led though the day. When her future in-laws poked and probed her, she swore her purity until they were satisfied. When an auntie put a plate on her lap, she forced the food down her throat. And when Rafael placed his hand on the small of her back or breathed in her ear, she fought the urge to crawl away.

The party went on well into the night, and Papa could barely stand by the time they got in the car. It wasn't the first time he'd driven like that, but it would be the last. And it was Fatima's fault. She had wished pain on them, and pain they had got. That had been her first thought when she woke in the hospital three days later and Sofia broke the news.

Mama and Papa were dead, and it was all because of her.

***

Silence stretched between Fatima and Sofia, a black hole filled with hurt and resentment. Sofia had tried to manoeuvre around it with small talk. Now, standing by the bay window again, she felt ready to dive straight into its vortex.

Perhaps it was the fact that Fatima had barely said a word since they'd met at the airport. Or maybe it was the way she held herself so tightly as she inspected the flat, eyes darting between half-finished paintings, fingers clenched into fists, in silence. Always in silence.

Sofia's was ready to slam her own fists into something, anything, so that she wouldn't have to listen to it anymore. She grabbed her Malboros instead and wasn't two puffs in when Fatima was by her side.

They took turns to blow smoke out of the window, settling into a pleasant rhythm. As if it hadn't been over sixteen years since they'd done this. The silence shifted. It no longer coiled around them, suffocating them under its crushing weight, but flowed peacefully, naturally instead. It awoke an old, deep longing in Sofia's chest. The kind of longing she thought she had vanquished when she left Granada. The kind of longing despised by someone who had fought so hard to create her own destiny.

She jerked away from the window, ready to leave the room, desperate for space. But Fatima's voice stopped her.

"I did a concert for La Paca's association," Fatima said, eyes still fixed on the busy road outside. "I… wrote a song for you. Would you like to hear it?"

***

Fatima married Rafael a year and a half after their engagement. She had spent that time in mourning, barely leaving her in-laws' house, no radio, no TV. No singing, either. That was the *gitano* way, and Fatima had embraced it gladly. Just like the wedding, it was a fitting punishment.

"It's not your fault," Sofia had pleaded. "You don't have to do this. Please, don't do this."

Fatima had said nothing. If words had eluded her before, now they simply weren't there. How can one explain such all-consuming guilt? Fatima was no longer Fatima. The parts of herself that made her so had retreated to a deep, remote corner of her mind. All that was left was a steely determination to make right by Mama and Papa. And so to her in-laws she went, leaving Sofia orphaned and sisterless. Her mourning meant she couldn't be at her sister's first exhibition, her graduation, her farewell party. Every milestone missed was a tally mark carved into the walls Fatima had built around herself.

Sofia tried to tear them down, but they remained. La Paca told her to give Fatima time. But Sofia had heard Fatima's song the night before the engagement, the one that wished pain on them all. Perhaps Fatima was simply fulfilling that wish, for Sofia had never felt such agony. And so, she built her own walls to keep it at bay.

The day Sofia left to start her new life in London, Fatima couldn't get out of bed, no matter how loud her mother-in-law's nagging or how harsh Rafael's threats. She knew it would happen. Everyone had been talking about it at the market and at church – the *gitana* who fancied herself a *paya*. The loose woman. The threat.

Walls couldn't keep the pain of Sofia's absence contained; it climbed over them, consuming Fatima, eating away at her flesh, her bones, her soul. The only way she could function was to retreat even further into herself, until she barely spoke, barely breathed. She watched her life go by from within like a spectator might watch a movie, one she's only half invested in, registering the twists and turns of the plot but never fully engaging with it.

It wasn't until a couple of years after, when her girls were only babes, that she tore the through the screen. And it was Sofia who prompted her. There was a picture of her in the newspaper. She was standing by La Paca, holding a beautiful painting of a *gitana* clad in a manila shawl. La Paca had launched her association to help *gitanas* access education. Fatima couldn't stop staring at the painting. The *gitana*'s haunting brown eyes burned with a fierce yearning, and the shawl around her neck was so tight, it dug into her skin. That was the future that awaited her girls if she stayed with Rafael. She knew it, the same way she had known when Sofia was gone – just like La Paca, Fatima had a knack for these things.

When the community ostracised her for leaving Rafael, La Paca welcomed her with open arms, helping her carve a life of her own and raise her girls to be respectful of their people's ways, but never at the cost of themselves. Just like Sofia had done.

Fatima had wanted to reach out, to explain. To apologise. But she had been quiet for so long, it had been hard to find her voice. Until now.

***

Fatima wove every sorrow, every regret into her soleá. It filled the space between them, piercing through the black hole's centre and shattering it.

When she was done, Fatima opened her arms, hesitantly, hopefully, and Sofia couldn't help but go to her. All the tension building inside her was released when she felt Fatima's fingers playing in her hair. A song couldn't make all the pain disappear, they both knew that. But it was a step in the right direction.

They wiped their tears and set out to bless the flat. Fatima brought a jar of water out of her suitcase, blessed by La Paca only the night before. Sofia made two bundles out of the rosemary sprigs and handed one to her sister. They dipped them in the water and sprinkled it around the home, chanting like Mama had taught them.

Romero, romero.

Rosemary, rosemary.

Que salga lo malo, y entre lo bueno.

Out with the old, in with the new.

And, as they blessed her home, settling into a peaceful, natural rhythm once again, Sofia closed her eyes and focused all her grown body's energy to the spot below her brow. When she opened them, the red line was still there, just as bright as it had been all those years ago, connecting her wrist to her sister's, like it always had.

Like it always would.

THEY ARE OF THE STARS – AN INTRODUCTION BY THE AUTHOR

Samara Wright

In my memory it was absolutely silent. Everyone gathered around the large windows, pushing forward, their faces turned towards the sky. The stars twinkled dimly. Threateningly. There must have been low whispers, crying, breathing, noises of daily life in the background; but when I look back, the crowds wait silently, hung between despair and misguided hope.

The news reports had been clear. There was no hope. Every scientist on the station seemed to have been called in to double and triple and quadruple check the results. They were coming, headed straight for us. It was simply a matter of time, not of escape.

When I think back to that last day – the adults replaced with strange giants, surrounding me as we all stare into space, the silence of the room, big enough to hold half the stations' population – it always seems more like a picture. The legs crowding me rising out of the floor like tree trunks. My arm straining up to reach my father's hand.

Strangers often ask me about that day. And I tell them this: the group of us, staring at the sky in silence, waiting. Usually they don't ask more. But there are the rare exceptions – those that savour the stories of horror and death, of catastrophe, of pain and sorrow.

I'm not saying that that's what you're doing by reading this book; not entirely. I'm sure there are those of you who do lust after the gruesome details. But I am not writing this for you. I am writing it for those statues, the giants, the dead. Perhaps for too long I have carried around these people's last moments with me. Perhaps they deserve to be known not merely as a statistic of humanity's conceited arrogance, but as people who hoped and dreamed – the people they were.

#

Before, well before all of it really, they were pioneers, heroes; a shining example of humanity's perseverance in the face of dire circumstances. They accepted every challenge as the first to take on life in space. They left their homes and families on Earth and made a place for themselves in the stars. They created new tools and technology and expanded our understanding of science. They are the reason the rest of us are still living; they pushed the frontier of the possible further and further into space. They became out first line of defence.

And they accepted every single risk to get to that point.

#

My father told me bedtime stories of the early days. I grew up completely surrounded with them. My friends and I built our own pretend spaceships, saving each other from meteors and, ironically enough, alien attacks. We mined the moons of Jupiter and space-walked to the neighbouring satellite communities.

Daily life among the stars was much the same as on Earth. We went to school during the day, our parents went to work, we cooked dinner, we played in artificial parks. And in some ways it differed: we rode monorails between the satellites, we had monthly emergency depressurization drills; I had never seen an ocean or mountain or sand. I never woke up with the sun in my eyes or really knew how the season flowed into one another.

My life had gone on in much that way for years, as life had years before me. Floating resolute in the silence of space.

And then a scientist looked out into the stars and saw the stuff of our nightmares.

#

Space is not 2D. There is no up and down. There was inside the station and outside the station. And outside the station was, in every direction and every way, an unforgiving, unstoppable force. My whole life I had heard the soft sounds of space rocks hitting the metal hulls. They sounded endlessly, harmlessly, just a part of life, like rain here on Earth. But slowly, these sounds grew louder.

Mistakes were made. No one sat me down and told me the exact reason for our impending doom. No one made me a flowchart. Even if anyone had bothered, I don't think we knew any more then, anything more informative, than the extensive investigations uncovered. We were clueless compared to the information available today.

They just messed up. All I knew and all that matters reduced to four words.

We began taking every suggested precaution; every recommended option, every proposed argument. The satellite populations evacuate to the main station, where everyone worked to reinforce hulls and windows. We began to construct a temporary habitat hidden on the surface of Ganymede.

And yet, we did not have enough: as though time, resources, and space itself had also turned against us.

A full evacuation should have been the obvious answer. Had we committed sooner…had we slept less…had we done more…. Hindsight can be cruel in that way. We thought we were too big to fail. Between the arguments and rechecked projections, what time we had wasted away.

#

The entire citizen population was entered into a lottery. Less than half made it to the moon habitat before conditions worsened. The rest of us had to take our chances on the station. The announcement still repeats through my nightmares: "make preparations".

Mostly I remember my mother crying.

She worked as a mission specialist and volunteered for emergency repairs requiring spacewalks. No one knew how long the attack would last and we couldn't afford a possible breach to go unchecked for even an hour let alone days.

The original idea was for the population to wait in their own rooms – if they had them – with the remaining satellite evacuees distributed between us. If we were needed, we'd be called. But a few hours before the first volley passed, almost involuntarily, we found ourselves, all of us, in the great hall under the fishbowl. We stood or sat together, staring at anything but each other's faces. Together and alone.

As the time grew near, one by one, we trickled over to the windows. One by one, with a sort of sick desired to see out own destruction, we waited, searching the sky. The stars stared back, witnesses.

When the first shots tore past, the crowds pressed forward and backwards simultaneously; those in the back reaching for a better view, the ones in front pulling away in panic. My father scooped me up out of the way, perching me atop his shoulders above the heads of the crowd.

More shots flew past, and I was turned away from the view. As people pushed against each other, my father slipped through the others. I twisted around to look one more time as we left the rest – friends, family – in the hall and headed towards the elevators.

#

My parents, as if gifted with foresight, had put in place a plan all of their own years before. During the day they went to work reinforcing hallways and airlocks, floating through the darkness outside the station, picked me up from school and baked cookies; at night, while I slept, they prepped a makeshift escape pod – stolen and stashed away from a cargo ship long before the station was even completed.

It was small, not really meant for long distance travel or extended periods of use. It should have been decommissioned and returned to scrap metal before my third birthday. It was definitely not prepared to outrun an alien attack the speed and size of the one bombarding us. But they had added to it, little by little, year after year, with scraps and odd bits left over from other jobs.

#

My father was running the moment the elevator doors opened. He didn't stop until he set me down in our rooms, slipping the straps of my brand new school backpack over my shoulders despite my protests. Then he told me one final story. He told me a story of a princess, alone and scared, but with an important mission. Her kingdom had fallen under attack and it was her duty to escape. She had to run as far and as fast as she could. And she had to be brave. With that, he pulled a syringe out of a drawer and put me to sleep.

He must have carried me through the hallways and the rising panic to their makeshift escape pod where my mother waited. They must have slipped me inside with my stuffed rabbit.

And then they saved me.

#

I wasn't there when the missiles finally ripped through the hull. I didn't wait through the fear and false hope of rescue my parents must have held onto for two days. I wasn't there.

I've seen videos. I've read every story and report and then read them again and again and again. I've seen the pictures of the after. The remains of the station. The singed strings of paper cranes floating among the debris and destruction. Some unfinished, floating alone, or, worse, in the hands of children. I could have easily been one of them.

But I wasn't there.

I wasn't in the habitat on Ganymede. I wasn't there while they watched what I did not. I wasn't there as the supplies dwindled and the shock faded and the full force of the horror settled in. I didn't wait day and night with nothing to do but watch the graveyard of stars.

I wasn't there when the rescue ships finally, finally arrived.

I've seen the movies and interviews and read memoirs. But I didn't live them.

I was asleep. Drifting towards the safety of Earth.

And I am ashamed to admit that when I did wake up, I was anything but brave. I had escaped, but for a long, long time, I wished I hadn't. I carried the weight of that statement with me every waking moment. I rarely slept. I sought out the survivors of Ganymede. And for a while we comforted each other. But the ghosts of the station, the images I wasn't there for, they never left me.

Even through the murky atmosphere of Earth I could feel the stars staring down at me – the only survivor of the station. They judged me somehow inferior to those of Ganymede, as if I took the easier way out. As if I *chose* the easier way. As if I didn't lose everything as well – even that choice itself. The stars gazed down on me at night and the ghosts followed me through the day. Years and years of waking nightmares flooded my vision, drowning me in the footage and recordings on loop in my imagination.

#

And yet, we adapt. Horror and sorrow eventually fade, leaving me with only the ghosts. The people that did not have escape pods, the emergency responders whose tethers snapped, those trapped behind airlocks, the ones that never made it off Ganymede, everyone my parents couldn't, didn't save – they remained.

I can't judge my parents' actions. They did what they did and I can't change the past. I don't know if they could have saved more with me. I'm not even sure how they died.

But I do know my father's bedtime stories. I turned to those stories of the heroes I left behind. I began to write. Not of the tragedy in the end – but of the victories and thrills of the beginning. The climb to success before the fall. The stories that everyone skips over in these introductions in a rush to judge the terrible end. The full story of the sentence that remains about their names on the memorial.

That's what *They Are of the Stars* is at its core.

It's a celebration of the ghosts.

It's a chronicle of those that dreamed.

It's a story of bravery at its finest.

Fresh Beginnings

Donna Foulis

Spring was finally underway. The promise of summer circulated in the fresh air, carrying the life affirming scent of new life from the budding leaves and awakening flowers. Ellie yanked open the tired old window to let out the stifling, stale air of her living room. She'd essentially been breathing the same air in which she'd snoozed, sweated and cried in for countless weeks now, but there was something about the way the sun winked at her that day that gave her the energy she needed to get rid of the stale atmosphere.

As she drank in the taste of spring, she took a proper look around the room. Papers were stacked in precarious piles, her clean laundry heaped up on the armchair. The wastepaper bin was jammed with empty wrappers, overflowing onto the granite surface of the fireplace and the sofa was dishevelled like it had been slept on and left to fester.

The impulse to tackle this mess niggled at her for the first time in weeks and for once she didn't feel like the effort required was simply too much to bear. She started with one thing at a time, folding the crumpled pile of clothes, finding that pair of jeans that she'd been vaguely hunting for the past 2 weeks.

Her phone bleeped to announce a message as she strode back and forth with piles of clothes to find proper homes for them, the bottom of the pile getting chucked straight back in the washing machine again.

Hey Ellie, how are you doing? Not heard from you in a wee while. You're missing out on some rather juicy office gossip… you won't BELIEVE what just happened. Xx

Nadine and Ellie were on the same wavelength when it came to work, most of the time. They were both 27 and had stumbled into boring jobs after University- the need to pay bills and eat dominating any thoughts of following their artistic ambitions of painting, writing and opening a transportable coffee-slash-gin stand. Several years down the line, Ellie had endured periods of binge drinking, daily gym visits, bursts of insomnia and in general, just a deep seated need to have SOMETHING to escape with, to make her switch off from the monotony of everyday reality. Whether that was focusing sculpting the perfect body, or knocking back cheap shots to forget her troubles, it still continued to eat away at her.

The pair of them survived the boring meetings, mind-numbing spreadsheets and office politics together. They got their tiny day to day thrills by making excuses to escape the office and gossip over coffee, and ranting about how pants their working days were, helping each other both disguise and survive hangovers at their desks. Nadine didn't succumb to the same sense of despair as Ellie though; she was perfectly happy to bitch about work, go out and get drunk and then continue with their weekly routine. Ellie on the other hand had become less and less able to just go along with things. It all coming to a head that One Day.

Ugh do I even want to know? All good thanks, hibernating like a bear. They hibernate right? Probs time to see the light of day in approx. 2 weeks. Xx

She began straightening up the sofa, shaking off the throw and punching some life into the indented cushions. The thought of going back to work and making small talk in the kitchen and pretending to care about targets and marketing plans and robotic emails gave her a stomach ache. It brought the memory of That Day, the tears, the running, the shouting, back into focus.

She took several deep breaths, defiantly stuffing the stray plastic wrappers back into the bin and stomping through to the kitchen to empty it.

Nooo I need a good chinwag over some wine like now. I miss you chick xx

She tossed the phone to one side, focusing instead on the task at hand. It was like she was really seeing the mess for the first time in weeks. It's not like she wasn't aware of it being there, but her mind simply didn't have the energy to really process it.

Fresh cup of coffee in hand, like a trusty sidekick, she glared at the stacks of unopened post and random bits of paper, *I will get the better of you lot, just you wait.* She perched on her knees in front of the potential avalanche and got to work. At first, it felt as painful as climbing a mountain with the added sting of having her eyebrows tweezed or having bitten into ice, to be confronted with the unpaid bills and reminder notices, but the more she ripped open the envelopes and confronted what was waiting inside, she began to feel the weight of it all ebb away slightly. She filed the things that didn't need further attention inside an empty Doc Martins shoe box, the rest she placed carefully on her desk.

Next up was the big box of random junk- it was filled with receipts, flyers, postcards and used post it notes. She flung much of it into the paper recycling pile, finding the odd little memento that went in the keep pile. In amongst her rummaging, she found a handwritten note that was addressed "Dear Ellie," in unfamiliar writing. She unfolded it and sat back on her heels to read the cursive scrawl:

Dear Ellie,

Thank you so much for hosting me- I had a blast! I couldn't imagine a better place to spend New Year or a kinder person to introduce me to your fabulous city.

What a great start to 2017- I'll be reminiscing about this time for years to come I'm sure and let's make sure that this is the year that we'll both make our goals happen for real, life is too short to not take chances!

A 5 star review is coming your way!

Amy x

She thought back to that night, over a year ago now. She'd been too broke to afford the gas bill so she'd rented out the sofa on online, praying that the tourist rush for New Year would enough to entice someone. Luck was on her side, and an extra £150 in her pocket, thanks to Amy and her spontaneous decision to travel to Scotland and experience Hogmany in all its boozy glory.

It was a particularly rocky time. The winter blues were in full swing. Her bank balance was like playing Russian roulette, her opponent having a sadistic sense of humour. One day it would lull her into a false sense of security and whisper *Go on, treat yourself to that pint. You deserve it.* Then the next day it would be filled with cynical laughter as it dropped all the charges it had processed on her, waiting for the worst possible moment to reveal this. *Oh luv, did you really think you could get the better of me? Let's not forget, I own you.* All her friends seemed to be doing lots of exciting grown up stuff; either jumping into their dream career, buying a house, getting engaged, adopting a dog, jetting off to the other side of the word… and there she was, too cold to afford heating and still unsure how to pay tax.

Everyone seemed to have their own thing going on for New Year and to avoid staying home alone and drowning her sorrows she signed up to be a bartender at one of the pop-up bars in exchange for £200 cash in hand. As a slightly eccentric lone traveller, Amy was filled with the buzz of excitement that comes from being on holiday and exploring a new city, despite the misery that Scotland called Weather. She got Ellie out of her pyjamas and fleecy socks and into the pub, waving a bottle of wine in her face before she could comprehend what was happening. This resulted in some quick, last minute planning for New Year's Eve. A time, a place, a back-up just in case they couldn't get in, and pre-drinks ready to be poured and necked whilst make-up, hair and dress decisions were made. They saw in 2017 in good spirits and a shared moment of friendship, more than the drunken disaster that Ellie had anticipated she'd become.

The next morning, she made pancakes, and her and Amy slobbed around in that hungover way, replaying the highlights of last night and spinning drunken antics into fully formed stories before the moments to remember were lost to the blackout power of alcohol. They tucked into the fridge full of Ellie's favourite comfort foods. She'd done a panic shop just in case her life fell apart as the New Year descended but instead of indulging in self-pity like she'd expected, they savoured it in their hungover state, reminding Ellie of the nights out they all used to have back in uni.

As Amy's departure approached, Ellie took it upon herself to brave the cold and take her new friend on a quick tour of her favourite night time sights: the emptiness of the castle courtyard, the far more beautiful sight of the cobbled streets of the Royal Mile under the glowing street lamps, the German market which was still going strong, despite the tired and cold faces manning the stalls and rides.

They hugged goodbye to each other with promises to stick to their New Year's resolutions, to stay strong and achieve all their goals.

How had an entire year passed and yet she'd still not achieved anything she'd set out to do? She re-read the p.s. scrawled at the bottom of the note:

p.s. the world, and me, are waiting for your book!

Ellie got up from the floor, shaking off the stiffness in her legs and boxed up the rest of the papers in one fail swoop, putting them away in the cupboard without ceremony. She padded through to the kitchen to pour a fresh cup of coffee, yanking open that window too to let the fresh spring air permeate through the flat and work its rejuvenating magic.

She stopped to take a moment to really breathe, leaning her forearms against the cold tiled surface of the window sill. The rooftops stretched out ahead of her and she thought about all the human beings who were enclosed in all these buildings. What were they doing? Did they too lock themselves away and doubt everything from time to time? Or were their rooms filled with people and laugher and light? It was impossible to ever know but mind boggling to imagine.

In dark times, she would always imagine that other people's lives were perfect. The snapshots of laugher she caught through the window of the pub down the street, the couples holding hands and wrapped up warm to battle the winter chill together. And there was Facebook. Filled with nothing but good news announcements and showing off epic travel pictures. Where are the days with rainy weather? Where couples bicker or party goers are too skint to go out. What about the days where people feel inadequate and unsure of their place in the world. Why do these things have to be such a big secret, surely it's all part of being human and simply living?

She heard the sound of her phone demanding her attention from the other room and picked up the coffee before padding back through to see what the darned thing wanted now. She closed the notifications that announced new Instagram stories and opened the email from her boss. It was a formal bunch of drivel about confirming her return back to work and Next Steps.

Just the idea of going back there made her heart rate start to rise and her breathing constrict. She tossed the phone back on the sofa and continued her purge of the flat, shaking out the dust and scrubbing and organising until it looked like a real home again, rather than an advert for hopelessness.

Another ding from the sofa revealed a text message.

Daryl says you're coming back soon- so happy that you're feeling better! Xx

Uh, when had she said such a thing? Of course the second he decides to make contact, without so much as a *how are you doing* that would be the decision made. Because she had no say in the matter of course. Nadine was just trying to be a good friend, she knew that. And of course technically she was coming to the end of her sick leave so they would be expecting to hear from her; but it was the image of slimy Daryl stampeding through the office and seeing everything in front of him through a money-making filter that got her riled up.

Actually, nothing is set in stone. I might take that trip to NZ after all. Xx

Her cousin had been angling for a road trip buddy on his New Zealand adventure, someone to read maps and budget and make sure they wouldn't starve between destinations. It would hardly be a glamorous couple of months but living in a van and experiencing a whole new country had to be better than spending her week repeating each day mindlessly at a desk. And as long as she had a pen, paper and the possibility of charging her laptop then there was nothing stopping her book from being written.

Rousing herself, she picked up the coffee and sat down at her desk, ignoring her phone and leaving it just where she'd tossed it. Switching on the laptop, she opened the word document that contained roughly a quarter of a novel, took a sip of coffee and finally began writing once again.

The Promises of Ghosts

Samantha Dolan

Marcus made a diamond in the space between his thumbs and forefingers and held it up to the sky. He sat alone on the stony river bank and with a squinted eye, tried to count how many stars were filling in his small aperture. There was Venus...Or a satellite. Or was it...? He dropped his hands and sighed. He should stop kidding himself he could name anything in the heavens. Even the phases of the moon confused him. But he was 23 years old, single, moderately intelligent and physically able to handle the journey. And such was the desperation of S.P.A.C.E since the disaster of the Emery, that those were the only criteria that mattered. For 50 years, Humanity had been travelling to the new world and now the last of the 7 Arc ships was embarking on their last journey to the stars. And Marcus was going with them.

The Survivor was an odd name for a ship, he thought. To him, it implied that it was being launched from a place of desperation not hope. When the first Arc, Endeavour, had launched all those years ago, before he was even born, yes, the Earth had been in dire straits. And so many of the population had died in famine or disease or war that a special craft had been constructed to send the 3.1 billion bodies into the Sun to avoid poisoning what was left of the world's resources. Marcus remembered reading about it at school and feeling uneasy when he learned the craft had crashed on Mercury because of an incorrect decimal point when calculating the effect of that planets' gravity. No efforts were made to retrieve it, the Powers-That-Be deciding the surface of Mercury was close enough, but it left a young mind wondering. How did every single person miss it? As an adult he realised that it wasn't so much that it had been missed but there was a great deal of passing the buck. People realised there could be a problem but were they certain enough to spend millions fixing it? Apparently not. And priorities shifted, the planet was down to give or take 4 billion people and would you believe it, the Earth started to recover. Government patted themselves heartily on the back, they had succeeded in rectifying the problem, now the human race could start to rebuild. Talk turned to the last Arc, Survivor and whether or not it should be launched at all.

Marcus sat in his living room and watched the debate with his parents, Abena and Theo and his best friend Rory. Rory threw nuts in the air and tried to catch them in his mouth.

"Bet you they take the thing apart and sell it for scrap" he muttered as another but bounced off his nose.

"They couldn't," Abena breathed clutching her non-existent pearls "we made a promise to the people who left…"

"…but everyone who actually left are long dead Mrs A." Rory stated. "And those that are on the new planet are barely human. By design! So. What do we owe them?"

Marcus felt his parents exchange nervous looks but he didn't speak. He looked at the prosthetic leg Rory had detached and stood beside him as a side table. Of course Rory wanted Survivor back, he'd never leave the Earth and that ship had the resources to make his life more comfortable. But for Marcus…his eyes wandered to the shrine of his great grandfather. The source of his hazel eyes. Grant Murray had been amongst the first to volunteer and the second ship to leave orbit. He'd taken his wife and children and given no thought to the woman he'd been bedding for 6 months. Marcus chose to believe he didn't know she was pregnant. Because he didn't want to think of the man GG loved so much as an arsehole.

Back in the room, he watched his mother's fingers flex in and out of prayer. Abena was right to be concerned. When the population hit 11 billion and the planet was dying and taking humanity along with it, of course petty differences were set aside and everyone worked together. There was one central Government who built the sky lifts and the platforms and the Arcs. There was a shared focus, a common goal. But now, the immediate threat was gone. Old divisions were starting to appear like cracks in a plastered wall. Eyes turned to whole vacant countries and tensions rose as people started to migrate towards them. Everyone was out for themselves, the shift imperceptible but gathering speed.

At the end of the debate, Government issued this directive:

It is decided by majority that the Survivor ship should first aid us with our repopulation of the planet. It will be sent on as agreed once it has serviced our needs.

Government decided to send a team up to Survivor to pillage. The Emery skylift, a Bastian of the old world, the pinnacle of technological advancement was commissioned to take a team of 700 scientists, engineers and doctors to decide what they couldn't possibly live without. Marcus was at work on the day the Emery launched from the Berlin station, attached itself to the Platform 1 pylons and started to accelerate into orbit where it should have docked 37 miles above the planet. Instead, Old Faithful rose majestically as it had done for over 40 years...And kept going. 700 people in a mythical great glass elevator smashed through Platform 1 and proved Newtons first law of motion.

Within the hour, Government issued this directive.

It is decided by unanimous decision that we will honour the Survivor treaty and will be taking applications for crew starting immediately. Special call for doctors and engineers and people of faith.

*

Marcus walked for miles with his mother on his last night on Earth. His father, a tight lipped man at the best of times, saw no reason to join them. He kissed his son on the forehead and breathed him in one last time. Then he turned on his heel and left. Marcus and Abena decided to hit the coast, allow the harsh winds battering the eastern Scottish coast to fill their lungs.

'I wish for so much,' she said, kicking pebbles from her path. ' But I will not ask you to stay. I fear...well, they say better the devil you know. But knowing this devil as I do I think it's best you leave.'

'What do you mean?'

Abena took Marcus by the arm and smiled at him. 'I mean, you and your generation, you've only ever known this. And you only understand this, this unity. And it's a beautiful thing but it cannot last. So go, you young ones go and fulfil the promise of ghosts while you don't know any other way of living. Don't wait until we teach you to hate.'

Marcus squeezed her hand and lost himself in her company. She often sounded much older than her years. He suddenly realised how much she had stood between him and the hard parts of the world. She was right, he didn't understand. As far as he knew, the entire planet was some kind of mixed race. It's just the way it was, no one ever said anything about it just as no one ever pointed out the sea was grey. Had he missed his mother's decimal point? He watched her stare into the middle distance and wondered what the consequences of his miscalculation could be.

"They're still looking for people to join the crew you know."

Abena chuckled musically "No, my son. My place is here. Your father would never leave the planet and there are enough of us up there I'm sure. Perhaps we will wander, settle in one of the new lands."

"You'd leave Scotland?"

"But why not? Not that I don't love it here. But this place, it's all about who I have been. I am curious to find out who I can be."

"Wow." Marcus whispered. "I always imagined you and Dad, right here. As you'd always been."

"Oh, but I'm not from here!" Abena laughed. "We are such a strange people. We travel great distances, drop our flag and say 'this is home'. And the way we fight to defend our home. Like beasts."

She stopped and fixed her son with a look of steel. "Don't fight for *things,* Marcus. Fight for the irreplaceable." She softened her gaze and started strolling again. "Now tell me, what will you do when you wake up?"

Marcus chatted to her, white lies about his ambitions for the ship because in truth, he had none. He didn't know why he was going. He had no desperate need to do so, he had no desperate need to stay. Crushed by the weight of choice he found himself frozen in place. So the idea of being told what to do, when to do it, what was expected of him, was appealing. But beneath it all he wondered about that bloody decimal place. Was *he* the miscalculation? What would 'close enough' mean on the other side of the known universe? What if, what if what if... Emotionally shattered, Marcus made his way to the Edinburgh lift. Rory strode confidently beside him.

"I heard your genetic match is placed right next to you. Is that true?"

"Not a clue, Rory. I've not been on board yet."

"Weird though, eh? That's the person you'll make the best babies with...on ya go son!"

Marcus glanced at Rory and sighed. "Yup, that's totally the way it's going to happen."

"What if she's been smacked by the ugly tree? Double bag her?"

"It's a real shame you're not coming with us, mate" Marcus snapped "what are we going to do without your insights."

Rory laughed. "Alright, I'm just trying to de-stress the atmosphere. You look like you're chewing on a wasp mate!"

"Yeah. Sorry. It's just...what if..."

Rory raised a hand to silence him. "It is what it is mate. You can run all the scenarios ya like. You can't know what's going to happen, you can't have a plan for any of it. You are leaving the sodding planet Marc. Whatever it is, you'll deal with it. Or you'll die. And that's it."

Marcus felt his jaw go slack at the simplicity of what he's just heard. Rory laughed harder and barged Marcus with his shoulder. "Get a grip, mate. It is what it is."

With a hug and a tear, the two friends parted ways and Marcus wafted in a haze towards his pod. He'd decided that he wanted to be the one to step foot on the new world, not just his descendants. He would be genetically modified in his sleep, along with the future mother of his children. But she hadn't arrived yet and he was relived because he was still processing what Rory had said. Ignoring the flippant 'get a grip' the man had a point. Marcus stripped down and went through decontamination, the air jets whipping over his skin like razorblades. The chemical wash stinging the newly exposed virgin layers. He was vaguely aware of the lack of human contact. The machines had taken over and the last vestiges of contact from his best friend had been blasted away with the rest of the earthly contaminants. But while Marcus felt alone, he didn't feel lonely. As the IV went in one arm, the sensors all over his body, the NG tube, the catheter and the bag installed, Marcus felt something almost like peace. The decimal place floated into his mind and out again, like the flash of lightening seared on his retinas and rebounding against his eyelids. If he thought hard he could stress about it, but it faded when he let go. And let go he did.

It is what is it he thought sleepily as the lid of his pod slid closed.

Contributors

Helen-Anne Ross

Danusia Staunton

Catherine J.Skye

After wrestling a Distinction out of her Creative Writing MA at the amazing Edinburgh Napier University, she has inflicted her short stories to unsuspecting audiences in live readings at literary events both in England and in Italy, and even had a few pieces shamelessly published on journals and anthologies.

She now lives in southern Italy, where she is allowed to vent her obsession on legends and folklore through benevolent magazines, and even occasionally teach in genre writing workshops and seminars. The latest project keeping her from finishing her first novel is a soon-to-be unveiled fantasy webcomic, Mystic Seals, with an all female gang of writers, artists and main characters - 'cause the internet just has no way of avoiding them.

Stephanie Bowman

Stephanie received her B.A. in English from BYU-Idaho and her M.A. in Creative Writing from Edinburgh Napier University. She specialises in writing YA fantasy but loves most genres. Much of her inspiration comes from her interests in astronomy, linguistics, ocean science, and interpersonal relationships.

Sim Bajwa

Sim Bajwa is a writer and bookseller based in the West Midlands. Her non-fiction has been featured in 404 Ink's Nasty Women and in Fiction & Feeling's Becoming Dangerous Anthology. Her fiction has been published in Helios Quarterly, The Dangerous Women Project, Shoreline of Infinity, and 404 Ink's Issue 4: Power. You can find her on Twitter at @simuella

Alexandra Balasa

Alexandra Balasa has been publishing in venues such as PodCastle, Deep Magic, and Cosmic Roots and Eldritch Shores. Currently she attends the University of Texas at Dallas, where she's a teaching assistant and PhD Student in literature and creative writing.

Samara Wright

Katy Lennon

Katy Lennon is a sci-fi and horror writer living in Edinburgh. Her work has been features in Shoreline of Infinity and 404 Ink's *The F Word*. She also runs the horror literary zine *Blood Bath;* details at bloodbathlitzine.com.

G.M. Barbour

G.M. Barbour is published as an entertainments writer, blogger, and reviewer under a different name, and is pursuing a career in YA fiction under a pseudonym. After completing an MA in Creative Writing and graduating with Distinction, they're currently seeking representation for their debut novel.

Megan Duff

James Ebersole

James Ebersole's stories and poems have appeared in such places as *The Horror Writers Association Poetry Showcase, Folk Horror Revival: Corpse Roads, Richmond Macabre, Werkloos,* and *Broken Worlds,* with work forthcoming in *Drabbledark* and *The Mammoth Book of Halloween Stories.* He lives in Northern Virginia and holds an MA in Creative Writing from Edinburgh Napier University.

Samantha Dolan

Samantha Dolan has been writing since she could hold a pen. She considers herself a genre fiction writer with a special focus on graphic novels and more recently, sci-fi. It's through sci-fi that she finds resolution. She graduated from Edinburgh Napier's MA in Creative writing in 2016 and now works with *Shoreline of Infinity* as the Reviews Editor.

Donna Foulis

Laura Gregory

Laura Gregory is a genre fiction writer and graduate of Edinburgh Napier University's Creative Writing MA. Her feet returned to Canadian soil, but her heart remains in Scotland. Working as a police records clerk, she fights crime by day and writes villains at night.

Lidia Molina Whyte

Lesley Macniven

Mother of two girls, coach and trainer Lesley Macniven completed her Creative Writing MA in 2018 during a career break. She is writing a non-fiction graphic novel exploring the causes of, and resolutions to, the glacial progress towards workplace gender equality told through compelling stories of women's lived experiences.

Olive Black - Illustrator

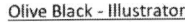

Printed in Poland
by Amazon Fulfillment
Poland Sp. z o.o., Wrocław